The New
BLACK
MASK

The New BLACK MASK

Number 6

EDITED BY

MATTHEW J. BRUCCOLI & RICHARD LAYMAN

A HARVEST/HBJ BOOK

HARCOURT BRACE JOVANOVICH, PUBLISHERS

SAN DIEGO   NEW YORK   LONDON

Editorial correspondence should be directed to the editors at
Bruccoli Clark Publishers, Inc., 2006 Sumter Street,
Columbia, SC 29201.

ISSN 0884-8963
ISBN 0-15-665485-7

Designed by G. B. D. Smith
Printed in the United States of America
First Harvest/HBJ edition 1986
A B C D E F G H I J

Contents

v

Georges Simenon:
An Interview

Simenon (he long ago reached the level of eminence that renders honorifics superfluous) was born in Liège, Belgium, in 1903, and writes in French. His most famous creation, Inspector Maigret, first appeared in 1931; but the many Maigret stories account for a relatively small portion of the bountiful Simenon canon. His work is superbly readable because—among other qualities —of its economy and pace. He has pared his prose to its essentials. Beyond readability, he provides accurate observation of behavior: what his characters do is what they are.

Simenon agreed to answer questions for New Black Mask in writing, explaining: "I am in the habit of writing 'short.' But I am incapable of long dissertations."

NBM: Certain critics insist that every great novelist has his own narrative "voice," and that this voice provides the defining quality of his prose. If you agree with this claim, please describe your prose voice. Is it consistent or does it vary with the different types of your novels?

Simenon: Naturally, every novelist has his own style. I have always tried to make mine as simple as possible, with a minimum of adjectives and adverbs, a minimum of abstract words which have a different resonance for each reader. I use a maximum of *mots matière*.

The rhythm alone varies according to the subject, sometimes from one chapter to another.

NBM: Are your characters' lives determined by forces—hereditary and environmental—over which they have no control? Or do you allow them the chance to alter their destinies?

Simenon: Very few people are capable of changing their destinies, but heredity, environment, and even climatic conditions play an important part in human behavior. A discussion between husband and wife on a lovely spring day will not have the same violence as in oppressive and thundery weather.

NBM: You have said that the purpose of your revisions is to remove the "literary" sentences. Yet you admire William Faulkner's work. Isn't he a highly literary writer?

Simenon: Faulkner was not considered as such when he started, so much so that he had to work in Hollywood to make a living, and if he was *largely* published and acclaimed in France, he had to discuss no end with his American publishers.

"Style is the reflection of man," and Faulkner was a most complicated person. Fortunately for us.

NBM: Most of your worldwide readers know your work only in translation and so have read Simenon filtered through someone else. What rules would you like your translators to obey?

Simenon: To safeguard my simplicity. Which is difficult, as for instance in Italian.

NBM: Are there elements in your work that are untranslatable?

Simenon: It depends on the languages . . . and on the translators.

NBM: What qualities should your ideal reader possess?

Simenon: To read without trying to *analyze*.

NBM: When you were writing a novel, were you consciously aware of technique—or did the material shape your technique?

Simenon: I have always searched after simplicity. Boileau wrote: When you want to say it rains, say: "It rains."

NBM: Did you see your characters' faces as you wrote about them? Did you deliberately collect or save the faces that you observed?

Simenon: I have collected, or rather, unconsciously recorded, living characters which I used, sometimes years later.

NBM: As the most widely read living author, do you feel that your work has "universal qualities"? If so, what are the qualities that cut across the borders, languages, and cultures?

Simenon: Simplicity? Sincerity? I just don't know.

NBM: If you were beginning your career in 1985 what kinds of novels would you try to write?

Simenon: I don't know. Probably the same.

The Man Behind the Looking Glass

GEORGES SIMENON

Translated by Harold J. Salemson

This marks the first publication in English of "The Man Behind the Looking Glass." The story was published as "La cage d'Émile" in Simenon's Les Dossiers de l'Agence "O" (Paris: Gallimard, 1943).

I

IN WHICH *a young lady swoons in the arms of sturdy Torrence, and in which we learn of the strange chain of command at the Agency.*

Eleven A.M. The viscous fog to which Paris awakened is the kind you can tell won't dissipate all day. The young lady has had her taxi stop in the Rue du Faubourg Montmartre, and dashes briskly into the Cité

Bergère. There must be a rehearsal going on at the Palace Theater, for two or three dozen showgirls and chorines are pacing back and forth on the sidewalk outside.

Directly across from the stage door of the famous musical-revue theater, a hairdresser's shop, its facade painted a gaudy purple: "Chez Adolphe."

To the right, a small door, a dark corridor, a stairway with no concierge to stop you. An enamel nameplate, these words in black on white: "Agency O, Third Floor Left."

The greatest of stage stars have gone through the portals across the street, and famous politicians, princes of royal lineage, and multimillionaires have been familiars of the Palace backstage.

How many of these same personalities, on mornings like this one, also sneaked in here, collars turned up, hats hiding their faces, up the stairs to Agency O?

At the third floor, the young lady stops for a moment and takes a mirror from her handbag. But not to check on her makeup. On the contrary, as she looks at herself, her face takes on an even more haunted expression.

She rings. A slow step is heard inside. The door is opened by a most unprepossessing clerk. The waiting room looks tacky. A newspaper on a small table. No doubt the clerk was just reading it.

"I would like to see the manager," she says excitedly. "Would you please tell him it's terribly important. . . ."

And she dabs at her eyes with her handkerchief. The clerk must have seen many more like her, for he turns without hurry toward an inside door, disappears, comes back a little later, and just motions to her.

The next minute, the girl goes into the office of Joseph Torrence, a former inspector of Paris' Criminal Division, now manager of Agency O, one of the most famous private detective agencies in the world.

"Please come in, mademoiselle," he says. "Have a seat."

Nothing could look more ordinary than this office in which so many terrifying secrets have been revealed. Nothing could be more reassuring than big old Torrence, an easygoing giant of a man in his late forties, looking very well groomed and well fed.

The window that looks out on the Cité Bergère has opaque panes. The walls are lined with bookshelves and files. Behind the mahogany desk, within Torrence's easy reach, the kind of safe you might find in any business office anywhere.

"Excuse me, monsieur, if I seem a little nervous. You will understand, as soon as I fill you in. . . . We're all alone here, aren't we? . . . I have just arrived from La Rochelle. All that happened there was just . . ."

She has not sat down. She paces back and forth. She folds and unfolds her handkerchief, obviously racked by the most extreme agitation, while Torrence methodically goes on filling his pipe.

At that point, a door opens. A tall redheaded young man, who seems to have grown too fast so that his suit has become too small on him, enters the room, notices who is there, apologizes, and says, "Oh, excuse me, boss."

6

"Well, what is it, Emile?"

"Nothing, monsieur. I just—I forgot something. . . ."

He grabs something, a file folder of some sort, which he has taken from one of the shelves, and disappears so awkwardly that he bumps into the doorjamb.

"Please go on, mademoiselle," Torrence says.

"I don't remember where I was. . . . Let's see. It was all so tragic, so terribly unexpected. . . . My poor father—"

"Maybe you better start by telling me who you are."

"Denise. Denise Etrillard, from La Rochelle. My father is the lawyer Etrillard. He'll be in to see you this afternoon. He left shortly after me. But I was so afraid I thought I'd better—"

Right behind Torrence's very ordinary office, there is another, smaller, darker office, filled with the most astonishing variety of things. The young redhead whom the boss addressed as Emile has sat down there at a common unpainted deal table. He bends down. He turns on a sort of switch and immediately he can hear clearly everything being said in the next room.

Facing him, a peephole. From the other side, no one would suspect the existence of this peephole, for it looks like a plain little mirror set in among the bookshelves.

Impassive, his eyes unmoving behind their big tortoiseshell glasses, an unlighted cigarette dangling from his lips, Emile is listening and watching, somewhat like the railway switchmen one sometimes sees perched up in their glass cages.

The young lady says, "Denise Etrillard. My father is the lawyer Etrillard. . . ."

Displaying no reaction, Emile has pulled a heavy directory to him. He looks through the list of lawyers, to the letter *E*—Etienne . . . Etriveau. . . . But no Etrillard?

He goes on watching and listening. This time, he is looking through a telephone directory, at the section covering the city of La Rochelle. There he finds an Etrillard, or rather, a Widow Etrillard, fishmonger. . . .

The other side of the looking glass, the voice goes on:

"I really don't feel up to giving you any complicated explanations right now. My father, who will be here by four o'clock at the latest, will be able to explain it to you much better than I can. It's so terribly unexpected. The only thing I would ask of you, in the meantime, is for you to put away in a safe place the documents I was able to rescue. . . ."

Emile grabs the phone in front of him on the desk. It rings in Torrence's office. Torrence picks it up and listens.

"Ask her what time she got into town," Emile is saying.

During this time, the young lady has taken from her handbag an impressive yellow envelope that looks even more important because of the five red wax seals that close it.

"Did you just arrive in Paris?" Torrence asks her.

"Yes, I hopped into the first available taxi and came right here. It was my father who told me—"

"Told you to come and see us?"

8

"We were just quietly sitting there, last night, when we suddenly heard noises in his office. My father reached for his gun. . . . In the darkness, there was a man, but he was able to get away through the French door. . . . My father immediately understood that someone was trying to get their hands on these documents. . . . But he couldn't leave La Rochelle just like that, without notice. So, as he was afraid they might come back again, he entrusted this envelope to me. . . . When he explains the whole thing to you, you'll understand why I am so nervous about it, so terrified. The people who are after us are absolutely ruthless. . . ."

During this time, redheaded Emile has kept right on going about his business like an obedient office clerk. After looking through the *Directory of Lawyers of France* and the telephone directory for the Department of Charente-Inférieure, he is now looking through the combined schedule of French railroads, without, however, taking his eyes off the girl more than a few seconds at a time.

Really quite good-looking, the young lady. She is dressed exactly the way a provincial young lady of good family should dress. Her gray tailored suit is cut to a perfect fit. Her hat is fashionable without being trendy. She is wearing pearl-gray suede gloves.

But there is one detail that Torrence is unable to see, because he is too close to her and it is difficult to examine as carefully as one would like a person who is talking to you.

Whereas Emile, at his microscope, as he likes to call his peephole . . .

If, as she has just said, she left La Rochelle in a hurry, if she sat up in the train a good part of the night, if she has only just arrived in Paris and taken a taxi from the railroad station directly here to the Cité Bergère, how does it happen that her suit, so simple and so absolutely proper, still has such neat creases in it, especially the creases in the sleeves that come from packing a jacket in a valise or trunk?

La Rochelle. Let's see, La Rochelle to Paris–Gare d'Orsay. . . . Well, the only train she might have come in on got to Paris at 6:43 in the morning.

"All I'm asking," she tells Torrence again, "is for you to put this document safely away in your safe until my father gets here. I beg you to do this for me, monsieur. He will explain it all to you. And I am sure that after that you won't refuse to help us."

She lies well. She is even very convincing. She paces back and forth. Is the nervousness she is displaying part of the act, too?

"Well, if you can assure me that your father will be here this afternoon," Torrence grudgingly assents. "But I would still like to have an address for you in Paris. Are you stopping at a hotel?"

"Not yet. I'll go and register at one now. I wanted to get here before anything else."

"What hotel will you go to?"

"Why—the Hôtel d'Orsay. Yes, right there at the railroad station. You'll keep this document safely for me, won't you? I imagine it will be safe, as long as you keep it locked up, won't it? No one would dare go after your safe, would they?"

She tries a pale little smile.

"No, no one would dare indeed, mademoiselle. And just to reassure you, I'm going to put this envelope in the safe right now, before your eyes."

That good old giant of a Torrence gets up, takes a small key out of his pocket, and opens the safe. Automatically, the girl follows him toward it.

"If you only knew how relieved I am to finally see these papers in a safe place!" she says. "The honor, the whole life of an entire family is at stake. . . ."

While Torrence conscientiously closes the safe again, Emile picks up the intercom once more, but this time he rings the desk of the clerk who is sitting reading his paper in the waiting room. Their conversation is short, if in fact it can be called a conversation. It consists of just one interjection of Emile's: "Get your hat!"

At the same time, the young readhead wrinkles his brow. The safe once closed, Denise has leaned falteringly against Torrence's desk, murmuring:

"Oh, I beg your pardon! I've been able to hold it all in until now. . . . But it was such a nervous strain. . . . Now that my job is almost done, I—I—"

"Are you ill?" Torrence is worried.

"I don't know. I—"

"Watch out!"

She has slumped into his arms. Her eyes are half-closed. She is gasping for breath, fighting off the fainting spell that is coming over her.

Torrence wants to call for help. She stops him.

"No. Excuse me, please. . . . It's really nothing. Just a silly moment of weakness. . . ."

11

She tries to smile at him, with a poor little smile that touches the heart of thick old Torrence.

"You'll be here at four o'clock, won't you?" she asks. "I'll come in with my father. He'll tell you the whole story. I am certain now that you won't refuse to help us out."

She is standing in the middle of the office. She bends down.

"My glove," she says. "Good-bye, monsieur, I can assure you—"

Barbet the clerk, whom they call by that name because the unruly hairs on his face are reminiscent of the bird so named, gets up to show her out the front door. As soon as she is out in the stairway, he dons a greenish derby hat, familiar to everyone in the Cité Bergère, puts on his topcoat and, going out through a different doorway, gets down to the Rue du Faubourg Montmartre before she does.

As for Torrence, he has turned toward the looking glass and merely winks. Emile leaves his own office and goes into the boss's.

"Well, what do you think of that young thing?"

To which the clerk with the suit that no longer fits him fires back in a tone that admits of no contradiction: "I think you are a damned fool!"

Anyone who ever set foot inside Agency O, anyone who in difficult or threatening circumstances ever called on the famous detective Torrence for help would be more than a little surprised if they could see him, shamefaced, head down, mumbling in confusion at the young man whom he introduces on some occasions as his clerk, on others as his photographer, and sometimes as his chauffeur.

It is true that Emile has now changed. Of course, his suit hasn't gotten any bigger or any less tight. His hair is still just as flamingly red, and he still has freckles around his nose and nearsighted eyes behind the tortoiseshell glasses.

Nevertheless, he no longer looks quite so young. Twenty-five? Thirty-five? It would take a pretty smart fellow to say. His voice is dry, cutting.

"What did you have in the left-hand pocket of your jacket?" he asks.

Torrence checks his pockets.

"Oh, my Lord!"

" 'My Lord,' indeed! If you think a young girl falls into your arms because she can't resist you. . . ."

"But, she was. . . ."

Torrence is crestfallen, appalled, humiliated.

"I beg your pardon, Boss. She finally had me feeling sorry for her. I'm just a damned fool, you're absolutely right. As for what she swiped from me . . . well, it's a catastrophe. We have to run after her. We have to find her, no matter what—"

"Barbet is tailing her."

In spite of being used to it, Torrence can't help being amazed, once again.

"The handkerchief, wasn't it?" Emile asks.

"Yes. You remember. I put it carefully away in an old envelope. I was figuring, this afternoon—"

"Open the safe, fast, you fool!"

"You want me . . . to open the—"

"Hurry, goddamn it!"

Torrence does as he is told. Despite his height and his girth, he is just a small boy when facing the thin young man with the glasses.

"Haven't you caught on yet?" Emile asks him.

"Caught on to what?"

"Take that envelope out of the safe. Put it on your desk. No, better still, put it on the floor. That's safer...."

Oh, come on! This time, the boss is really overdoing it. Torrence can't see how an envelope that may at most have a dozen or so sheets of paper in it can . . . It's true that there are small-sized bombs, but none as small as that, surely. . . .

"I just hope she doesn't give Barbet the slip," Emile comments.

That beats all. Torrence is bug-eyed. Give Barbet the slip, indeed! As if anyone has ever succeeded in ditching Barbet!

"Do you remember, Torrence," says Emile, "the definition of a good corporal? Big, strong, and stupid. Well, if things go on like this, I'm afraid you'll be making corporal soon!"

"What can I say to that?"

"Nothing. Just tell me what we did this morning."

"The insurance company phoned at eight o'clock, to put us on the trail of—"

"How many times has that happened in the last six months?"

"I'd have to check my calendar for that. Maybe twelve or thirteen times—"

"And what did we find each time we got to the site?"

"Nothing."

"What you mean is, we found a jewelry shop that had been burglarized. Always the same modus operandi. . . . A man lets himself get locked into the building the night before. A man who laughs at locksmiths however smart they may be, and knows how to outfox every burglar alarm ever invented. Who does a neat, flawless job. Up to now, what kind of traces has he left?"

Torrence looks like a schoolboy who hasn't done his homework, his forehead turning every shade of red.

"No trace at all."

"And what about this morning, at the jewelry shop in the Rue Tronchet?"

"We found a handkerchief."

"Doesn't that mean anything to you?"

Torrence slams his fist painfully down on the top of his desk.

"What a fool I am! A damned fool! A goddamned fool!"

"Don't you smell anything?"

Torrence sniffs. His broad trencherman's nostrils beat the air like the wings of a bird.

"I don't smell a thing."

Two or three times already, Emile has looked over at the phone, with a worried expression on his face.

"I just hope Barbet . . ."

For six months now, Agency O has come up empty-handed. Six months during which the largest of the insurance companies specializing in insuring jewelry

15

has called in the Agency, the police having gotten no-where. And during that period, thirteen burglaries. Without a trace. Without the tiniest clue.

And this morning . . . Torrence and redheaded Emile, lugging heavy photographic equipment with them, had gotten to the spot at the same time the police got there. There was a crowd outside the window of the jewelry shop.

"Boss, I'm sorry," Emile had called out. "Could you lend me a hand reloading the camera?"

Torrence came over. Emile whispered to him:

"Under my foot . . . a handkerchief. . . . Be careful."

Torrence, doing as he was told, dropped something and, bending down to pick it up, grabbed the handker-chief. A little later, when no one was watching him, he slipped it into an envelope and put the envelope into his pocket.

Who could have seen what he was doing? Someone who was outside the shop perhaps, in the mob, among the two or three hundred gapers.

In the taxi, coming back to the Cité Bergère, they had taken a look at the handkerchief. In the corner, there was a laundry mark.

Emile said, "Now we've got them. This after-noon, Torrence, start making the rounds of Paris laundries. . . ."

The phone rings.

"Hello. . . . Yes. . . . Where? At the Four Sergeants? Well, then you have lunch, too, old man. What else can I tell you? If, by any chance, you make the mistake of letting her get away. . . ."

Then he explains to Torrence:

"Your young lady from La Rochelle is right now sitting in the Restaurant of the Four Sergeants, at the Place de la Bastille, and she just ordered lunch. . . . Don't you still smell anything?"

"I think I'm catching a cold, boss."

"But that shouldn't keep you from seeing. . . ."

On the floor, a thin wisp of smoke is coming up from the yellow envelope. Torrence wants to rush and grab it.

"Just let it go, Old Man," Emile says. "It's just as I thought."

"You thought the envelope was going to burn up?"

"If not, there was no reason for her to be so insistent that we lock it away inside our safe."

"I must admit—"

"—that you don't understand. Well, it's not so hard to figure out. *Someone* saw you pick up the handkerchief and slip it into your pocket. *Someone* immediately understood that we finally had a clue, and since the reputation of Agency O is rather well established, *someone* got scared. What time did we get back to the office, Torrence?"

"At ten-thirty."

"And at eleven, in walks this Denise. Where could the handkerchief be at that time? Either it had remained in your pocket, or else you had put it on your desk, or, even better, being a cautious man, you had temporarily locked it away in the safe. Look. . . ."

This time, a small flame is licking out of the envelope, and then, in a few moments, it has burned up with all the papers that were in it.

"There you have it! If that envelope had stayed in our safe, by now everything in the safe would have been destroyed by the flames. A little trick that chemistry students learn. You dip some blotting paper into a certain kind of chemical solution, and after a given amount of time in contact with the air, it bursts into flame.

"While the young lady from La Rochelle was spinning her tale for you, and you were falling for her line, she was pacing back and forth in your office and taking in every last detail.

"You opened the safe, and she leaned forward and looked right into it. She didn't see the envelope with the handkerchief.

"There was a very good likelihood that the thing was still in your pocket. So she had to put on another little act, playing the damsel in distress who faints and hangs on to the shoulders of her nice fat savior."

"I'm not so fat as all that," Torrence protests.

"Nevertheless, she succeeded in doing it, and while she was in your arms she got the handkerchief back, and if that brute of a Barbet is unlucky enough to lose her. . . ."

He takes down his topcoat and hat.

"I'd better go look into this myself."

"You want me with you, Boss?" asks poor cowed old Torrence, looking like a whipped dog.

And yet, throughout the world he is considered one of the greatest of detectives.

II

In which grape scissors are used for something other than cutting grapes, and in which a rum punch suddenly finds itself put to an unexpected use.

All the customers have left, one group after another. The restaurant is practically empty. Now it just smells of stale cooking, wine, and coffee.

Over in a corner, near the door, Emile has dismissed Barbet, after having taken his meal with him, a most copious meal, in fact, for they were serving snails, and he consumed two dozen of them. It is unbelievable how Emile, long and lean as he is, can do away with food, especially the heaviest kind, the hardest to digest, the kind that scares off the strongest of stomachs.

"Go back to the office," he told Barbet. "Tell the boss I don't know when I'll be back."

Did he overeat? Or was the half-bottle of Bordeaux getting to him? He made sure to order a black filtered coffee. But, of course, he counteracted that with a shot of the house's best cognac.

Across the room from him, the young lady from La Rochelle has taken a gold cigarette case out of her bag and lighted an Egyptian cigarette. They are looking at each other, across the empty restaurant between them. There is still a bit of sawdust left on the floor. The help have started straightening things, sweeping up, changing tablecloths, but the two of them still sit there, getting in the way, and it is already 3:00 P.M.

When he got there, Emile did not try to pull any

tricks. He just went straight over to Barbet, who was sitting in his corner, trying to hide behind his newspaper.

"How are you?" he asked. "How did she get here?"

"Taxi. Too bad!" Barbet sighed, for, had the girl taken the Métro or a bus, or even just walked a short way on the street, he would have been able to find out what was in her handbag.

Barbet, under an earlier name that was well known to the police blotter, was once a renowned pickpocket. He even ran a school over near the Porte Clignancourt in Montmartre, using a dummy with bells on that the pupils had to frisk without making them tinkle.

But now he had gone straight. Why? Well, that was nobody's business but Emile's and his own.

"Did she make any phone calls? Did she meet with anyone?"

"No. Except that she did go down to the ladies' room. I followed her to the door. But I couldn't decently go in there with her."

She was looking at them, and Emile was sure she had recognized him. Considering that she barely got a glimpse of him at the Cité Bergère office, she was surely the one who was in the crowd earlier this morning outside the Rue Tronchet jeweler's.

Oh, well! There are some people with whom there's no point in playing games.

"You can take off, Barbet."

Now she and he are alone in the restaurant, separated by the breadth of the room, and at times it might almost seem they are smiling at each other.

So much so that one of the waitresses, getting impatient, says to her partner: "I wonder why they're beating around the bush like that so much. Why can't they just decide and go to it, for goodness' sake! They'll end up that way anyhow. . . ."

At 3:10, Emile asks, with a sort of shyness he almost always displays in public, an exaggerated politeness that goes well with his looks: "Would you be kind enough to let me have another cognac, please, mademoiselle?"

Across from him, the girl who claims to have come from La Rochelle, calls out in turn: "Would you please bring me some grapes? And a rum punch!"

"Flaming?"

"Of course, flaming."

She is served the grapes with a pair of slightly curved scissors. The waitress strikes a match to light the rum, which lies in a dark layer at the top of the glass.

Then the girl, deliberately, after taking a good look at Emile, withdraws a handkerchief from her handbag, cuts a corner of it off with the scissors, and places that bit of material in the flaming alcohol.

"What are you doing?" the waitress sputters.

"Nothing. Just a recipe of my own."

And she smiles at Emile, with a come-on smile. Emile gets up and walks across the restaurant.

"Do you mind?" he asks.

"Please do," she replies. "Mademoiselle, bring monsieur's glass over to my table."

And a moment later, in the kitchen, the waitress is all smiles. "See? What did I tell you? Putting on such airs! And they end up the same way as any other two!

Why the hell don't they go ahead and do it? Just get out of here! Do whatever they want, as long as they let me get on with my polishing. . . ."

"I do not believe that we have had the honor of being introduced to one another, have we?" she says.

And so saying, she blows a mouthful of smoke in his face. He, on the other hand, has turned his face slightly away, out of consideration, for he is thinking of those two dozen snails that were literally bathing in garlic.

"Unless, of course," he replies, "you really are the daughter of the lawyer from La Rochelle."

She laughs. Relaxes. Oh, well! She also realizes that she is no longer dealing with Torrence, and that this is no time for playing games.

"Not too much damage to your safe?"

"The envelope was taken out in time."

"Was your boss, Torrence, the one who figured it out?"

"Monsieur Torrence," he answers in an elocutionary tone, as if reading from an advertising brochure, "is a man who sees all, knows all, and thinks of everything."

"But still is not sharp enough to know when his pockets are being picked. You know, I'm beginning to think that maybe you were hidden someplace in that room, and that maybe you are the one who . . . But let's get down to the business at hand. Are you planning to stay here all afternoon?"

"I don't especially relish the idea."

"Let's lay our cards on the table, shall we? First, it

was your bearded little sidekick who started tailing me. You came to spell him. From what I've heard about Agency O and the cases it has successfully solved, I know it would be childish for me to consider ditching you through a house with two exits or by changing trains on the Métro. You lost the first round, but you've come right back in the second."

"I don't understand," he mumbles, all innocence, the picture of the man who gets slapped.

"You had the handkerchief. I got it back. Incidentally, I don't mind giving you what's left of it. The laundry mark is gone in my drink. So, now you are in charge of tailing me. And by the same token, I can't go anywhere at all. Some fun!"

"To tell the truth," he sighs, "I don't find that so distasteful."

"Maybe you don't," says she. "Mademoiselle! My bill, please!"

"Both together?"

"I should say not! Monsieur can settle his own."

What would Torrence say if he saw her like this? No longer the young lady at all, or at least one heck of a sophisticated young lady. And yet, still with what might be called a kind of distinction, something or other one rarely comes across among people the police, or even private detectives, usually deal with.

"You never more talkative than this?" she asks.

"Never."

"Too bad. We're keeping these waitresses from finishing their jobs. Settle your bill and let's get out! I suppose it doesn't matter to you which way we go?

That being the case, let's walk down toward the Seine. It's quieter there."

They do not know that their waitress has just lost her bet. She bet her cronies that they would see the couple head straight for the first hot-sheet hotel of the Rue de la Bastille. Instead of which, they are walking quietly off along Boulevard Henri-IV.

"What you would like to find out, come hell or high water," she says, "is where I'm going, where I came from, and who I was working for this morning, eh? That's it, isn't it? You followed me. You'll go right on dogging my footsteps. And for my part, I am determined not to give you any information; in other words, not to go back home and not to have any contact with any of the people I know."

She turns toward him, irritated, and then bursts out, "But why the devil don't you light your cigarette?"

"Oh, I'm sorry. Just an old habit. I never light it."

She had thought this would be an easy one, and yet she has never met so impassive a fellow as this tall red-headed young man who follows her around with such exceptional determination.

"Well then, why do you keep it in your mouth?"

"I don't know. If it really bothers you . . ."

"Why do you try to pass yourself off as detective Torrence's photographer?"

"I beg your pardon. What do you mean, pass myself off?"

"Don't try to kid me. This morning, you were strapped up with a big camera. You were pretending to take pictures. But you forgot to take the cap off your lens. . . ."

24

He smiles and acknowledges the point.

"One for you."

"What do you do at that agency?"

"I work there."

"And you're most certainly underpaid."

"How do you know?"

"Because you wear ready-made suits that shrink when it rains."

They have reached the Ile St.-Louis. She sighs.

"I wonder what I'll do with you. Not to mention the fact that I'd sure like a chance to change my clothes."

"I don't doubt it."

"Why do you say you don't doubt it?"

"Because you put that suit on in a hurry, at the last minute, so that you didn't get to take the creases out of the sleeves. You usually dress more carefully than that, more luxuriously, I imagine, because you didn't change your stockings, and you're wearing stockings that go for a hundred and ten francs a pair. A little high for the daughter of a provincial lawyer."

"You an expert in stockings?"

He lowers his eyes and blushes.

"At any rate," he says, "your accomplice or accomplices are expecting you, and they're beginning to be worried. I wonder how you'll be able to get a reassuring message to them, with me on your tail. You'll also finally have to find a place to sleep. You'll have to—"

"Happy prospect!"

"Yes, I was just thinking the same thing."

They automatically watch a string of barges that a tug is dragging upstream.

"Moreover," Emile goes on, with his congenital

25

humility, "if you don't sleep in your own bed, we'll know it by tomorrow. . . ."

She shudders, looks at him, and says, "Fill me in on that."

"Considering the point we've gotten to, it would be gauche of me to turn down such a request. Just follow my reasoning for a moment. If the handkerchief that was lost at the jewelry store during the burglary was sufficiently damning evidence to move you to do what you did this morning—"

"Oh, hurry up! It's freezing out here."

"I was saying, there are two kinds of laundry marks. Those that are made for private customers; they're not very compromising. But modern laundries have a very huge clientele. That's why they use special markings for the laundry from the large hotels—"

"That's stupid!" she cuts in.

"Just the same, it made you turn pale! Anyway, I suppose that you and your accomplice or accomplices live at some hotel, probably one of the large hotels. The laundry mark would have put us on your trail. Now it's just part of a punch that nobody, I hope, will try to drink! I say, if you don't mind—on account of those snails that I ate—would you object to stopping at this little bar to have a beer at the counter?"

She follows him condescendingly.

"Two draft beers!"

"That still hasn't clued me in on why, if I don't sleep in my own bed tonight—"

"Well, you saw that I sent my colleague away."

"The one who looks like a duck-hunting dog?"

"That's right. He, and a few others, will now undertake a bit of real deep research. Tomorrow morning we will have the names and descriptions of all the women in your age group registered in any Paris hotels who did not spend the night in their own rooms. To your health! . . . Patron, how much do I owe you?"

"I asked you a question a little while ago."

"Did you? I don't remember it."

They are again walking along the river.

"How much do you make, working for Agency O? What would you say to—"

"That would depend on how much you have on you."

Taking him at his word, she opens her bag. They are at the tip of the island, where you can look up at the Cathedral of Notre Dame. The fog has lightened.

"If I were to give you—"

She counts the bills. Thirty . . . forty . . .

"—Fifty thousand francs?"

She is beside herself with joy. No way that this poorly dressed young man, who looks like an impoverished clerk, can refuse such a fortune.

"All you have to do is miss the subway train I get on. . . ."

"But then," he answers calmly, "you won't have any cash on you. No, you won't! Fifty thousand francs is all that you have in your purse. What if you don't meet up with your accomplice? What if he got scared, and has already taken to the hills?"

She can't keep from smiling slightly.

"You turning me down? Isn't it enough?"

"It's too much and not enough. I'm not very good at figures. The job you pulled off last night brought you some eight hundred thousand francs' worth of jewels. The one last month, on the Rue de la Paix, two million. The one on the Boulevard Poissonnière—"

"I'm asking you one last time: YES or NO?"

Then, falling all over himself with gallantry, he whispers, "I'm just enjoying your company too much."

"You'll be sorry."

She pretends no longer to pay any attention to him. She crosses the bridge, hails a taxi. He climbs in right behind her, without waiting for an invitation. The cab stops in front of a fancy boutique on the Rue St.-Honoré.

"I don't imagine you expect to—"

"Oh, I love women's clothing," he assures her.

He follows her from department to department. When she reaches the cashier's desk, the salesgirl asks:

"Where should we send the purchases?"

And she gets a sudden bright idea and blurts out, "Just give them to my husband's valet here."

Shoes. Silk stockings. From time to time, she looks sarcastically over toward him, but he is not the least bit fazed and hangs on to the packages, except when he has to wipe off the lenses of his spectacles.

"Haven't you had enough yet?" she demands.

"Oh, it doesn't bother me. It's just that the taxi won't be able to hold it all."

Five P.M. Six P.M. The taxi driver, when they have

him wait at a particularly crowded intersection, looks daggers at them and follows them to the door of the store.

"What hotel? Well, let's see. Hôtel du Louvre."

And, at the hotel, she asks for a room. Emile keeps behind her.

"Twin beds?"

"No. A single. Just for me," she replies.

"And for you, monsieur?"

"Nothing for me," Emile mumbles.

She is exasperated. Up in the room, the packages piled up on the bed, she is almost livid with fury.

"How long are you going to go on like this?"

"I think it would be best if we went down to the bar for a cocktail. They have an excellent American bar in this hotel," Emile replies.

"Oh, now you're an expert on bars, are you?"

"Just as much as on silk stockings, Mrs. Baxter."

That is the name under which she registered at the hotel.

"And even more of an expert on jewel thieves. You are really making a mistake in not coming to join me for a Manhattan."

She follows him, flabbergasted. It is hard to picture the self-effacing Monsieur Emile in an American bar, yet he seems completely at his ease there, even correcting the bartender on the proportions for the cocktail.

"As you can see, my little lady."

"I forbid you to call me 'my little lady.' "

"As you can see, my good friend."

She opens her mouth as if to protest again, but she

realizes she'll never have the last word with him. Even if he were slapped in the face till he was red as a lobster, trampled on, cursed out ferociously, he would never lose any of his cool or his strange self-assurance, the latter all the stranger for being accompanied by such amazing apparent modesty.

"You are young," he goes on.

"What about you?"

"Me? Oh, if you only knew! Anyway, you have selected the toughest trade to follow, the one that on the surface pays the biggest dividends, to be sure, when you consider the value of the jewels. But what risks you run! . . . And besides, how much can you get for stolen jewelry from even the most honest of fences, if there are any? It's so tough a trade that only a few of the rare specialists ever make a go of it, and the police are on to all their ways of operating. . . ."

"Do you mean that last night's burglary—"

"Last night's burglary and the twelve jobs before it here in Paris during the last few months . . well, I would have sworn to you, until just a few days ago, that they had to be the work of Baldhead Teddy. . . . Bartender! Let us have another round, please!"

"Why do you say you would have sworn they were, until just a few days ago?"

"Well, because I—no, excuse me, my boss, Monsieur Torrence, who is a most extraordinary man in his own way, was smart enough to contact the New York police and found out that Baldhead Teddy was still in jail. The answer just got to us yesterday. But there's no doubt about it."

"Do you have any proof that I'm not Baldhead Teddy, or an accomplice of his?" she sneers.

"Baldhead Teddy, little girl—"

"Before, you called me your little lady."

"Yes, and I might even get to just calling you 'little one'! Now, drink up. Baldhead Teddy, as I was saying, never worked with any accomplice, either male or female. The only jewel thieves that ever got away with it, the ones that might be considered of international stature, have always worked alone. But Baldhead Teddy carried that policy to an extreme of perfection."

She laughs, icily.

"You sound like a schoolteacher."

"A country schoolteacher, right?"

At times, she can no longer be sure. There is about him such a strange mixture of humility and pride, of authority and modesty. And his eyes . . .

"What do you think," he asks, "is the most dangerous time for a jewel thief?"

"You seem to know more about it than I do."

"It's when he sells the jewels. All valuable jewels have an identity, a description by which they can be traced wherever they go. That is why Baldhead Teddy never went in for pinch-penny jobs. When he pulls a heist, it's on a grand scale. For three months, or maybe six, he robs the jewelry stores of just one city, say, Paris, London, Buenos Aires, or Rome. He does a neat job, quickly completed, and always done in the same modus operandi. But just as long as he stays in the country he is in, he makes sure never to flog a single one of the stolen jewels.

"Baldhead Teddy, in his way, is a wholesaler. He has enough capital to be able to hold on for a while, as the common saying goes. When he's accumulated enough loot, he disappears. No more trace of him around. The international police forces are all alerted to his possible resurfacing, but no dice.

"He makes his sale very far away, say, on another continent, and much, much later. Baldhead Teddy then has enough on hand to be able to live peacefully for several years. I would bet that somewhere in the world he is known under a different name, honored and respected, perhaps even the mayor of his town or village.

"And then, when he starts running out of money, he makes plans for a new campaign. He takes a six- or twelve-months' leave of absence. . . ."

Emile downs his drink and orders some more.

"So!" he concludes, "if the American police did not vouch to me—oh! I mean, didn't vouch to my boss, former Inspector Torrence—that Baldhead Teddy is currently behind bars, well, I for one would swear that—"

At that moment, something unusual happens. The young woman puts her hand on his wrist, and questions him:

"Just who are you?"

"Don't you think I should be the one who is asking you that? You know I'm just a legman at Agency O."

"Well, if the legmen are all like you, I wonder what the boss would be like."

"So do I."

"But, then, if you are the boss, why do you try to pass yourself off as—"

"Look, at the point we've reached—and I've now drunk three Manhattans, not to mention two cognacs at the Four Sergeants and that beer in the café on the Ile St.-Louis—at this point, I might as well confess that this is my own modus operandi. If, this morning, I had been the one who had interviewed you—"

"I would not have felt at ease with you."

"Perhaps so. Or else, I might not have felt at ease. As you know, I'm really quite shy, and—"

"And me trying to buy you off with fifty thousand francs!"

"Do you have any idea where we might go to have dinner? I saw that you bought an evening gown. You're really lucky to be such a perfect model size. But if we are going to dress, I'll have to take you home with me, and you'll have to wait with Mother while I—"

"Tell me, Monsieur Emile."

"What?"

"If you could, would you send me to prison?"

The young woman's lower lip is trembling. She feels she looks her very best. She can see her reflection in a mirror, between the bottles behind the bar. Her eyes are shining, her lips alive. And isn't her companion, sitting next to her, showing just a bit of interest in her?

She is awaiting his answer, her fingers tensed. It comes at her like a pebble.

"Without batting an eye."

"Don't you have any heart at all?"

"My father, mademoiselle, was killed by . . . Never

33

mind, it's not the kind of story to tell here. I might add something more, if you think it would help keep you from doing something foolish. In case you were to attempt to ditch me, I wouldn't be afraid to shoot you in the leg—and a very beautiful leg it is. That's how convinced I am that you were involved in the burglaries that—"

"Pig!" she hisses at him as she kicks him in the shin.

"And now," he asks, "are we dressing for dinner or not? Do I phone Mother to tell her to get my tuxedo ready, or do I—"

"You certainly don't expect to stay in my room while I change, I hope."

"Unfortunately, that's just what I do intend. But, if you wish, I can be closed off in a corner near the door, behind a screen."

Five minutes later, they are in the hotel elevator, on the way up to suite 125.

III

In which Torrence makes a discovery and in which a certain young lady suddenly turns as talkative as any detective could hope.

"Mother, while I'm dressing, will you please be good enough to keep an eye on mademoiselle," Emile says, "and make sure she does not go out or communicate with anyone."

It is a comfortable apartment, as middle-class as can

34

be, on the Boulevard Raspail. Emile's mother is as tiny as he is tall, and it is a sure thing that her hair, now gray, was never red. As if it were the most natural thing in the world, her son has put his gun in her hand. She acts as if she doesn't know it is there. She smiles to her young lady guest and treats her with utter politeness, without the slightest trace of irony.

"Please have a seat, mademoiselle. Can I get you something to drink? So, it seems you are a friend of Emile's. . . ."

Five minutes later, the latter is ready, and he kisses his mother on both cheeks, takes the gun back from her, and sticks it in his pocket.

"Now, if you're ready, we can go out to supper," he says.

Not much later, they are inside The Pelican, on the Rue de Clichy in Montmartre, where there are already couples dancing among the tables to the strains of a Cuban band. Emile has lost none of his shy look, yet he orders their supper like a connoisseur.

"Would you ask the gentleman over there to come over and talk to me?" he asks a waiter.

The gentleman is Torrence, also dressed in a tuxedo, his shirtfront overly starched, looking very flushed, at a small table the other side of the dance floor.

"Will you excuse me, mademoiselle?" Emile says to her, without ever taking his eyes off the girl. He and Torrence stand talking a few feet away.

"I followed your instructions," Torrence tells him. "I started with the better hotels that aren't too luxurious. I showed the doormen and concierges our picture

35

of the little bird. At the sixth hotel, the Majestic, on Avenue Friedland, it was met with surprise.

" 'I thought that she was up in her room,' the concierge told me.

"He phoned the room.

" 'Strange!' he said. 'Now I see that her brother has gone out, too. He should be back any time now, I think.' "

And Torrence goes on.

"I asked them to call together the whole staff that worked that floor. The couple are registered as Dolly and James Morrison, of Philadelphia. The girl was in room 45 and her brother in room 47. The rooms have a communicating door between them. As far as I could find out, James Morrison keeps very irregular hours, didn't come home to sleep last night, and they haven't seen him since."

"Any luggage?" Emile asks.

"I didn't dare ask that, in front of the whole staff. So I took room 43, *telling them that I had my own personal valet with me.*"

His wink clearly informs Emile that the valet in question is none other than the hirsute Barbet, and that the latter, right now, is probably very busy riffling through the two adjoining rooms.

"As soon as you hear something, let me know," Emile tells him. "Here or elsewhere. If we leave The Pelican, I'll leave a message for you."

"Excuse me, Miss Morrison," he says as he comes back to their table. "A few instructions I had to give to my

36

boss, as you can see. How is the caviar? Is it good and fresh?"

She does not seem particularly taken aback by the new information about her he has just acquired. On the other hand, her eyes bug open when he adds, "Torrence expects to have a really good talk with your brother James tonight."

"Does he?"

"At the moment, one of our friends has taken James in tow. Torrence is going to join them, and I have no doubt your brother will gladly come across with the information we want."

She looks down into her plate. She sighs. "Poor Jim!"

"Yes, it may be a little tough on him, indeed. Would you like a little more caviar? Some lemon on it?"

"Listen to me, Monsieur Emile."

She is nervous and edgy.

"I never expected you to get to the bottom of this so fast. I can't understand how my brother could have been so careless as to . . . Oh, well, let me ask you a question first. Just how are you involved in this case?"

"One of the largest insurance companies, which has been a client of ours for a long time, has hired Agency O to get back the jewels stolen in the thirteen jewel robberies that have taken place in the last few months."

"Nothing more than that?"

"What do you mean?"

"I mean that, since you don't actually belong to the police, you are under no obligation to turn anyone over to them, are you?"

Dancers passing near them, couples having supper at

37

other tables could have no idea of the tenor of this conversation being carried on with pursed lips.

"My brother is a jackass," the girl goes on. "I was sure he would end up getting us in trouble. Just this morning, I had to take it on myself to keep that marked handkerchief from remaining in your hands."

"How about a dance?" Emile asks, to his companion's great amazement.

But what is more amazing is that he is a most accomplished dancer. They continue their conversation on the dance floor which is bathed in orange spotlights, and the girl has the feeling that her escort is hugging her to him more insistently than the occasion demands.

"You weren't completely off the mark before, Monsieur Emile, when you talked about Baldhead Teddy. You thought you saw his fine hand in these jobs, and there's a good reason for that. I am Baldhead Teddy's daughter. Jim is my twin brother. Until now, our father has always kept us outside his acquisitive activities."

They go back to their table and champagne is served.

"Where we were living is of no importance. But you must know that Jim and I were raised and lived like the son and daughter of a very good family. Recently, our father was arrested in the States. This was the first time the police had ever been able to nab him. And that was only through an unusual set of circumstances. Jim and I thought that if we could just get together some money, we might probably be able to get Dad out of prison. So we came to Paris, and—"

"And you carried on right in your father's footsteps," Emile chimes in.

She smiles weakly.

"You can see that we didn't really get away with it. Jim had to go and lose his handkerchief on the last job. I saw you through the shop window. I wanted to . . ."

Her eyes have misted over. Her lips tremble a little; she takes a sip of champagne.

"I don't hold it against you," she goes on. "Each of us is just doing their job, right? What does scare me is to think of Jim going to jail. He's such a delicate boy. When we were kids, I was always the tomboy of the two, and he was more like a girl. What was that?"

"Nothing. I didn't say anything."

"That's why I asked you that question about the police before. Even if he is really arrested, Jim won't be able to tell you where the jewels are, because I'm the one who is in charge of hiding them. If you promise me that you will let him go, I'll turn them over to you. You will have accomplished your mission, and I can promise you on my end that, this very night, Jim and I will be out of the country."

She has stretched her hand out across the table and is touching Emile's.

"Be nice," she whispers, with a very engaging little moue.

He does not withdraw his hand from hers. He is embarrassed and, as on any such occasion, he ends up by slowly, punctiliously, wiping off the lenses of his spectacles.

"Are the jewels at the Majestic?" he asks, after clearing his throat.

"You don't beat around the bush, do you? If I answer you, how do I know that you'll keep your promise?"

"Excuse me! I haven't promised anything yet."

"Are you refusing then? Do you think you are going to get Jim to talk? You don't know him, believe me. He is more stubborn and obstinate than a woman, and besides . . . What time is it, anyway?"

"Eleven-thirty."

Well, well! Why does this fact seem to make her even more nervous than before? Could this be the time that her brother James should be coming back to the Majestic, or else . . .

"Would you like to dance this number?" he asks.

"No, thanks. I'm getting a bit weary. Besides the fact that I'm concerned about my brother and that . . . Would you pour me another glass of champagne?"

Her hand is trembling nervously. Emile is holding the bottle in his. He leans across the table. The last thing he sees is the look in the girl's eyes, which he is very close to, and it seems to him that they are sparkling with ironic enjoyment.

He does not have long to think about that. At that very instant, the room is plunged into darkness. Waiters can be heard scurrying about. Couples are bumping into one another and laughing about it.

"Don't move, mesdames and messieurs. Don't panic. Just a moment's patience, please. We merely blew a fuse."

Emile tries to grab hold of his companion, but his hand meets nothing but air. He gets up and walks straight ahead, toward the door and the stairway, but there are people who unintentionally stand in his way, and when he tries to shove some of them aside, they protest.

"Where does that one think he's going?"

"What a brute!"

The lights go on again. Dolly is nowhere to be seen. Come to think of it, is she really Dolly, or Denise, or some other name? Emile goes down to the cloakroom.

"Did you by any chance see a young lady who—"

"You mean the one who just stepped outside because she was feeling faint? I wanted to give her her coat, but she said no, she was just going out for a few breaths of air."

No trace of Denise-Dolly outside either, naturally. Emile, bareheaded, in his tuxedo, is standing on the virtually deserted sidewalk, near the blinking sign of the Casino de Paris, when a taxi pulls up. Torrence comes out of it.

"Where did he go?" he demands.

Emile knits his brow. Wondering what has gotten into Torrence.

"Did you let him get away, Boss? You know what we discovered going through the baggage? That the brother and sister are one and the same person! Only one of them—a man, obviously."

"Or a woman," Emile replies.

"At any rate, a very sharp article."

"That's what comes from behaving with modesty," sighs the redheaded young man. "While she was changing her clothes at the hotel, I stayed primly behind my screen. That gave her time to write a little note. Once she got here, she probably slipped it to the maître d' or one of the waiters, with a hefty bill attached to it. 'Please turn out all the lights, for just a moment, at exactly eleven-thirty.' And that was when she asked me to pour her some more champagne, so I would have the bottle in my hand."

Torrence makes no comment. Perhaps he is not totally unhappy to see that even his strange boss could fall into such a simple trap. At long last, he presumes to ask, "Are you sure she didn't pick your pockets?"

IV

In which Torrence is upset by his boss's lack of activity and in which the latter nevertheless finally does give some orders.

Three A.M. at the Cité Bergère. Torrence has boiled some water on an electric hot plate and made them coffee. Emile is lying on his back, stretched out on a narrow couch, just staring at the ceiling.

"What I don't get, if you want me to tell you how I really feel about it," Torrence finally says, "is that you're not even going over to the Majestic to have a look-see. I admit that Barbet doesn't often overlook any kind of clue. And I've been over everything myself, too. . . ."

Emile does not react. Impossible to tell whether he even hears Torrence's voice. It would almost seem he doesn't.

"In a word, where do we stand now? We just know that the burglar, whether a man or a woman—"

"A woman," Emile cuts in dolefully.

He does not feel he can add that when they were dancing, a few hours before, he held her so tightly in his arms that he had no doubt at all that she was a woman.

"Okay, if that's the way you want it. As I was saying, we have the proof that the jewel robberies were committed by a woman, that this woman had registered at the Hôtel Majestic under the name of Dolly Morrison as well as her brother James, which must have been a very practical arrangement. Because that way she could sometimes go out as a young woman and at other times as a young man. No one, in a hotel the size of the Majestic, would think of being surprised that they never saw the two of them together. As for knowing whether she is really the daughter of Baldhead Teddy —well, whatever she is, she slipped through our fingers. There is just one question left, the only one that still matters: Where did she hide the jewels? Because we can be sure that she will eventually go wherever the jewels are. We have the Majestic under surveillance. There was nothing to be found in either of their rooms. And she didn't deposit anything in any of the hotel safes, either."

Emile comes back in a dreamy voice:

"You certainly are talkative, Torrence, for a policeman."

"And you are certainly apathetic! I'm beginning to wonder whether you realize that time is going by. It's true that I've given the police the picture of our sweet little crook, and right now they have every railroad station and every seaport covered."

"Listen, Torrence, if you go on beating your gums like that, I'm going to go and lie outside on the landing."

Now, let's see. . . . Inasmuch as . . . Because of Torrence's volubility, Emile has to keep starting his reasoning over from the beginning. Inasmuch as this woman has committed thirteen jewelry-shop burglaries; inasmuch as she can afford two rooms in a large Paris hotel; inasmuch as none of the jewels has been sold; inasmuch as they quite apparently are nowhere in the hotel. . . .

"Give me a cup of coffee, will you, Torrence?"

What was it that Baldhead Teddy did in such a case? This is something we don't know, for he never discussed his modus operandi with anyone. But one thing at least Emile is sure the girl was not lying about: She really is the daughter of Baldhead Teddy. And she may very well have undertaken this series of burglaries to amass enough money to buy her father's way out of jail.

It all makes sense. *It has the ring of truth.* . . .

Very well! Then, now she is in Paris. She pulls off her first job successfully, the one on Boulevard de Strasbourg. Then the burglaries follow one another, on an almost weekly basis.

What does she do with her loot? That is the main question.

What does she do with the jewels until she has gotten together enough of them to meet her needs, so she can go abroad and sell them?

As if he were himself following his boss's train of

thought, Torrence announces while preparing another pot of coffee: "She must have another pad someplace in Paris."

"I would lay money she doesn't."

Why? First of all, because she is too smart for that. And also because she is using the modus operandi that her father, *who was caught only once during a whole long career*, perfected with the utmost care.

And besides, even though Baldhead Teddy has been in prison for several months now, the police in the States have not yet come up with any of the jewels he stole!

For another thing, at her room in the Majestic, they found a valise with a secret compartment in the bottom, and in it a full set of burglar's tools. If the girl had any other Parisian home, she would probably have left that compromising equipment there.

"Would you mind sitting down instead of walking back and forth like a bear in a circus?"

"I'm just trying to keep from falling asleep," Torrence groans. "If we have to spend the whole night here..."

Now, let's start all over again. This time, Emile does his thinking in the first person. He becomes the girl in question. He becomes the jewel thief. He has just pulled off his first successful job. He has the jewels in his pocket. They are not very cumbersome. He has taken only the most valuable stones, preferably only diamonds....

What will he do with them?

A large wrinkle creases his forehead. He is still staring at the same spot on the ceiling as if it were an obsession.

Necessarily, indispensably, these jewels must remain in a safe place for weeks on end, if not for months. . . .

Necessarily, indispensably, if by any accident I am arrested, or followed, or if my whereabouts are discovered . . .

He feels he is getting close to the truth. Yes, he's got it! She may come under suspicion; she may be tailed; her luggage may be searched; but what matters *is that no proof against her can ever be found.*

"Do you get it now, my little Torrence?"

Little Torrence, towering at six feet two over his skinny boss, looks at him wide-eyed.

"Do I get what?"

"How many branch post offices are there in Paris?"

"I don't know. Maybe a hundred."

"What time is it?"

"Four-thirty in the morning."

"Would it upset you very much to have to wake up the Superintendent of the Criminal Division? You know he'd never turn down a request from a former associate of Inspector Maigret's. Ask him to lend us for an hour, later this morning, just as many men as he can spare. You can't imagine how urgent it is that this be done right away. The post offices open at eight o'clock, don't they? Well, at each one of them . . . Yes, that's it, I knew you understood. Let each man have a picture—just the head—no clothes. No, I don't think I want any more coffee. Now, I'm going to get me some shut-eye, in the meantime. . . ."

Paris begins to come to life. The fog has turned liquid, changed into a fine, freezing rain. The streets seem lacquered with it. A man who is still grumpy and sleepy at that very moment appears at each of the branch post offices, which the clerks have just opened.

"Criminal Division. Could you tell me whether recently a person that looks like this photograph . . . ?"

Emile is snoring. One would never imagine that so skinny a young man could sleep so noisily. It is just before nine o'clock when Torrence shakes him awake.

"Boss! . . . Boss! . . ."

"Where?" Emile asks, immediately in command of his senses.

"Dunkerque. Hôtel Franco-Belge."

"Quick. The phone!"

"The hotel?"

"Yes, the hotel, and also the Dunkerque police. Get a move on!"

They are both still dressed in last night's tuxedos. The shirtfronts have lost their stiffness, and their beards have grown out. Torrence, moreover, has scattered ashes from his pipe over everything. The place smells like the morning after an all-night party, with dirty cups and bits of croissants lying around on the desks.

"Hello, operator, would you please connect me with number 180 in Dunkerque. And right after that, with number 243. Yes. Priority. Official business."

Emile has gone back into his little office. He really is a directory freak. Let's see, Dunkerque. . . . It was eleven-thirty when she got out of The Pelican. Okay.

47

No train to Dunkerque before 6:30 A.M. So, she couldn't have gotten there yet by train.

On the other hand, what if she had gone by car? He checks the mileage on a road map, and does some quick mental arithmetic.

The phone rings.

"Boss! It's the Hôtel Franco-Belge."

"Hello! Is this the manager's office? You say the manager isn't there yet? You're the cashier? This is the police speaking. . . ."

No need to specify it's just a private detective agency.

"Listen, madame. During the last few weeks, you must have received several small packets addressed to one of your guests, a Madame Olry, didn't you?"

The cashier repeats the name.

"Madame Olry? Wait a minute, I'll have to ask. I don't handle the mail. . . . Jean! Has there been any mail to hold for a Madame Olry? . . . What? What was that? . . . Yes, monsieur. You're right. It seems she is a lady who writes to us from abroad and asks us to hold her mail for her here. . . . Jean! Where did the lady's letters come from? . . . Just a minute, monsieur. . . . What was that, Jean? From Bern, Switzerland?"

And then her voice comes back stronger on the phone.

"From Bern, monsieur. It seems that several small mail packets have arrived for her. . . . Just a moment, madame. . . . Jean, would you please take care of madame?"

Intuition or what? Emile goes pale.

"Please don't hang up! Madame! Cashier! . . . Tell me, weren't you just talking to a woman guest of the hotel?"

"Yes, monsieur."

"A woman who just drove up by car?"

"Just a minute. I'll look and see. . . . Yes, monsieur, there is a car outside the door. It's a Paris taxi. . . ."

"Please don't talk so loud, madame, for the love of God! And don't talk so much! Just listen to what I am saying. You must not let that woman get away. She is probably going to ask you for the mail you are holding for Madame Olry. It is absolutely imperative that you—"

"You think she is Madame Olry?"

"What a fathead!" Emile shouts, in a rage.

The cashier, who has no idea what this is all about, sticks her foot into it as if it were the most natural thing in the world. Of course, she immediately turns to the woman across the counter from her and asks,

"You are Madame Olry, aren't you? I just have someone on the line, who is—"

"Shut up, for heaven's sake!"

"What? I can't hear what you're saying."

"Of course not! What is your new arrival doing now?"

"Wait a minute. I'll call her back. Madame! Say, there, madame! . . . What in the world? . . . Jean, run after that lady and ask her if she . . . Hello? Are you still there on the line? Would you believe it? The lady has got back into her car. . . . Yes, Jean? . . . You say the cab has left? . . . Hello! The cab has driven away, monsieur. Tell me, what am I supposed to do now? If someone comes to collect the packages, what am I to do?"

"Where are they?"

"I don't know. Probably over in a desk drawer, where we keep the hold-for-arrival mail. We get a lot of that."

"Madame, you are to lock those packets in your safe immediately. You are not to deliver them to anyone. Do you hear? Not to anyone. If the lady comes back . . . But I have no fear of that. After what she heard, she's not likely to come back. No, she surely won't come back, madame. Good-bye, madame."

When he hangs up, his eyes look wild. He wipes his brow. He slumps down on a chair.

"If I could only put my hands on that jackass of a cashier!"

And Torrence, who has understood none of it, asks, "What's going on?"

"We had her in our grasp! While I was on that phone, she was there in the lobby of that hotel. She had just come in from Paris, by taxi! A few seconds more and she would have claimed the mail that was being held for her. All we had to do was have the cops come in and pinch her. I knew I wasn't on the wrong track, that I couldn't possibly be on the wrong track. *It just had to be a hotel near the border*. Do you get it, Torrence? Simple as how-do-you-do. After each burglary, the jewels went off in a small packet, not even by registered mail, addressed to one Madame Olry.

They went to a hotel right near the Belgian border. That way, in case of any misstep . . ."

He takes a cigarette from his case, but as usual, he forgets to light it. He is calming down, little by little. He even ends up breaking into a smile.

"She really must have wondered how I was able to . . ."

It was at one and the same time an agreeable and an exasperating feeling: the feeling of having struggled against someone who was very strong, of having met one's match.

And, in this case, nobody lost!

To be sure, Emile had located the jewels, and that was all that the insurance companies wanted. But then Dolly . . . Was she Dolly? . . . Or was she Denise? . . . In a word, the girl, by now, had had time to make it across the border.

He would probably never see her again.

How would she remember him?

How would he remember her?

"What do I do now, Boss?" Torrence wants to know.

"You'd better phone the insurance company. Ask them to have someone go to Dunkerque with you. You will tell them that . . . well, that last night, thanks to your personal modus operandi and the unparalleled organization of Agency O, you discovered—"

"The head of the Criminal Division will want to know what became of the girl."

"Well, just tell him the truth. Tell him you haven't the foggiest!"

At that moment, the doorbell rings. Barbet is still

staking out the Majestic, so he isn't there to answer. Emile himself goes to open the door, forgetting that he is still wearing his tuxedo.

"You want to see the boss? Who shall I say is calling? Just have a seat. I'll go in and see if he is free."

After the Thin Man: Conclusion

DASHIELL HAMMETT

In Part One, Nick and Nora return to San Francisco from New York to find a welcome-home New Year's Eve Party in progress at their house. The party is interrupted when the body of the former gardener for Nora's family is mysteriously deposited on the doorstep. Later that night, Nick and Nora visit her Aunt Katherine for dinner. There they find Nora's cousin Selma distraught over the disappearance of her husband, Robert Landis, and Nick is browbeaten by Aunt Katherine into trying to locate him. Nick and Nora go to a known hangout of Robert's called the Li-Chee, managed by Dancer, where they find Robert in the company of Polly Byrnes, the club singer, whom, he tells them, he plans to marry.

Soon afterward Robert, who is very drunk, leaves with Polly; they are followed by Phil, who is described as Polly's brother. Outside, Robert meets David Graham, long enamored of Selma, and accepts a bribe to leave her. He agrees to go home for the last time to pack his clothes.

When Robert arrives home, Selma protests his leave-taking and pulls a gun. As he walks into the foggy night, he is shot to death. David arrives out of the fog, takes the gun, and throws it into the bay. Back at the Li-Chee, having gotten word of Robert's murder, Nick has arranged to have the police meet him in Dancer's apartment.

DANCER'S APARTMENT—at the Li-Chee. Nick is lying on the sofa, as before. Lum Kee is sitting in the corner, reading a book. In another chair, Polly is sitting, manicuring her fingernails. Dancer is sitting astride a chair, chewing a toothpick and looking angrily at Nick. Nick is in the middle of an apparently long and pointless anecdote.

Dancer spits toothpick out on the floor and says angrily, "Listen, we're putting up with you, but do we have to put up with all this talk?"

Nick sits up and looks at him in surprise, saying "But I thought I was entertaining you."

A Chinese waiter opens the door and says, "Mr. Caspar here—"

Caspar comes in. He is a little man, almost a dwarf, sloppily dressed, with bushy hair, and is addicted to Napoleonic poses. He comes into the room bowing and smiling to everyone and saying "Well, well—what is it?"

Dancer, grouchily. "Do I know? So a guy comes in and buys a drink. He goes out and somebody kills him. What are we supposed to do, give the customers insurance policies with the drinks?"

Nick says, "Wouldn't be a bad idea—with the kind of stuff you're serving."

Caspar advances toward Nick with his hand out, saying "I didn't recognize you for a moment, Mr. Charles. You remember me—Floyd Caspar?"

Nick says, "Oh, yes," and pats his pockets as if to make sure he hasn't lost anything.

Caspar goes on, "A man killed! Surely you don't

think these people—" he looks at the three others in the room as if they were saints, "—would have anything to do with a thing like that!" He puts a hand on Dancer's shoulder and says, "Why, I've known this boy since he was—"

Dancer pushes the hand off roughly and says, "Save it for the district attorney. What're you wasting your voice on this gum-heel for?"

Through the closed door comes the sound of men arguing. Then the door is swung open by Lieutenant Abrams, pushing a Chinese waiter against it. Two other detectives are with Abrams. He looks very tired and very dissatisfied with all the people in the room. When he sees Caspar, he groans and says, "I knew it would be like this. I knew there would be some shyster around to slow things up."

Caspar draws himself up to his full five feet and begins pompously, "Lieutenant Abrams, I must ask you—"

Abrams pays no attention to him, walks over and sits down on the sofa by Nick, asking not very hopefully, "Is it right you know something about what's been happening?"

Nick says, "A little."

Abrams says, "It can't be any littler than anybody else seems to know. Do you want to say it in front of them—or do we go off in a corner?"

Nick says, "This suits me."

Abrams asks, "Is this the dame Mrs. Charles was telling me about—that lives in Dominges' apartment and was with Landis tonight?"

Nick says, "Yes. She sings here, but she took time off to see that he got home all right."

Abrams says gloomily, "She certainly did a swell job." Then he asks Polly, "And what did you do after he got home?"

Polly says, "I came back here. I work here."

Abrams says, "When did you find out he was killed?"

Polly says, "After I came back—maybe half an hour. Dancer told me. I guess Mr. Charles told him."

Abrams says, "Never mind guessing. . . . I guess you know your landlord was killed this afternoon?"

Polly exclaims, "What!"

Nick says, "I told her earlier tonight, but she seemed to think it had to do with some fellow named Peter Dufinger, or Duflicker, or something."

Polly says, earnestly, to Nick, "I honestly didn't know, Mr. Charles. I never knew what his name was, except Pedro."

Abrams asks, "What did you know about him besides that?"

Polly says, "Nothing. I've only lived there a couple of months and I never even seen him more than half a dozen times—"

Abrams asks Nick, "You believe her?"

Nick says, "I believe everybody. I'm a sucker."

Abrams asks Polly, "Who do you think would kill Landis?"

She says, "I haven't the faintest idea. Honest I haven't."

Nick says, "Miss Byrnes has a brother who carries a gun. Dancer was chucking him out when I came in. I hear he hung around for a while outside. . . . Perhaps until just about the time that Polly and Landis left."

When Nick says "Dancer was chucking him out," Polly looks sharply at Dancer, but when Nick finishes his speech, Polly jumps up and comes over to him, saying earnestly "Phil didn't have anything to do with it, Mr. Charles. He wouldn't have any reason."

Nick says, "I'm not accusing anybody. I'm just talking." Then he tells Abrams, "Dancer says he threw him out because he was bothering Polly for money."

Polly turns to Dancer, angrily exclaiming "That's a lie! You had no right to—"

Little Caspar interrupts her, saying "Take it easy—take it easy. That's the idea of this police clowning—to get you all at each other's throats. Just answer any of their questions that you want to and don't let 'em get under your skin."

Abrams complains to Nick, "That's the way it goes. I leave that little shyster stay in here because I got nothin' to hide and he keeps buttin' in. If he don't stop it, I'm going to put them where he'll need a court order to get to them."

Caspar smiles and says, "Well, that's never been much trouble so far."

Abrams turns to Polly again, asking "Where is this brother of yours that didn't kill anybody?"

Polly says, "I don't know. I haven't seen him today."

Abrams asks, "Does he live with you?"

Polly says, "No. He lives in a hotel on Turk Street. I don't know just where."

Abrams says, "You don't know much about anybody, do you?"

Polly says, "I honestly don't know what hotel. Phil's always moving."

Abrams says, "What's the matter—does he have to move every time he don't kill somebody? What does he do for a living—besides not killing anybody?"

Polly says, "He's a chauffeur, but he hasn't been able to get much work lately."

Abrams asks if anybody knows a Selma Young. Nobody does.

Abrams asks Nick, "What do you think of it now?"

Nick says, "My dear Lieutenant, you wouldn't expect me to question a lady's word."

Abrams says, "It's all right for you to kid. Nobody jumps on your neck if you don't turn up a murderer every twenty minutes." He sighs and, indicating Dancer and Lum Kee, asks, "Well, what about them?"

Nick says, "They seem to have disappeared not long after Polly and Landis went out. Then showed up again with their hats on around the time I heard about the murder."

Abrams asks Dancer, "Well?"

Dancer says, "I went out to get some air. What city ordinance does that break?"

Lum Kee, who has continued to read all through the scene so far, puts down his book and says, "I went with him."

Dancer tries not to show surprise.

Abrams says, "Yeah? Where'd you go for all this air?"

Lum Kee says, blandly, "Air pretty much same every-where. We go in my car—ride around. Ask chauffeur."

Nick says, "There was another little point: I told Dancer Landis had been killed, but he seemed to know that he'd been shot."

Abrams asks Dancer, "How about that?"

Dancer says, disagreeably, "This is the twentieth century—in a big city. How do most people get killed—battle axes? I just took it for granted, like you would when you don't know you're on the witness stand."

Abrams asks, "Have you got a gun?"

Dancer takes an automatic out of his pocket and gives it to Abrams. From a card case he takes a slip of paper and gives it to Abrams, saying "Here's my permit."

Abrams asks Lum Kee, "You?"

Lum Kee brings Abrams an automatic and a permit.

Caspar says, "If you're going to take those, Lieutenant, we should like a receipt."

Abrams complains to Nick, "I can't stand that shyster."

Nick. "I was beginning to suspect that."

Abrams asks Polly, "Have you got a gun?"

Polly shakes her head no.

Abrams. "What'd you do with it?"

Polly. "I never had one."

Abrams, wearily. "Nobody has anything, nobody knows anything. I don't see why I don't give up this racket and go farming."

Dancer, to Caspar. "Everybody thought he did a long time ago."

Abrams. "I'm laughing. Did you know this Pedro Dominges?"

Dancer. "No."

Abrams looks at Lum Kee, who says, "No."

Abrams stands up wearily, saying "Come on, we're going down to the Hall of Justice."

Caspar. "On what charge?"

Abrams, disgustedly. "Charge, me eye! Witnesses. You ask 'em questions—where were you when you were over there?—and you have a stenographer take it down. You ought to know. Your clients spend nine-tenths of their time doing it." He looks at his watch, nods at the door through which the sound of music comes, says, "Or maybe for staying open after hours. Didn't you ever tell 'em about the two-o'clock closing law?"

Caspar. "I'm going with 'em."

Abrams. "And you can bring the wife and kiddies for all I care."

The door opens and Nora and David come in accompanied by a detective. David and Polly look at one another with startled recognition, but neither says anything. Nora goes quickly over to Nick, who asks, "What are you up to now?"

Nora. "Have they found out who did it? Who did it, Nick?"

Nick. "Sh-h-h, I'm making Abrams guess."

Abrams looks from David to the detective and asks, "Where'd you find him?"

Detective. "You told me to shadow anybody that left the Landis house. Well, Mrs. Charles did, and went over to his apartment, and I knew you wanted to talk to him, so as soon as I found out who it was, I went on up and got him. There's something about a fellow on the fire escape, but they can tell you better than I can."

Abrams looks questioningly at Nora, who says, "Yes, it was—" She looks at Polly, hesitates, says, "It was her brother." Then to Dancer. "The one you threw down the stairs when we came in."

Everybody looks expectantly at Polly, who seems dumbfounded. After a long moment she exclaims, "I don't believe it!"

Nick says, "That's certainly a swell answer."

Abrams asks Nora, "What was he doing on the fire escape?"

Nora. "I don't know. He went away as soon as we saw him, and by the time we could get the window open there was no sign of him. You know how foggy it is. And then this man came"—indicating the detective—"and by the time we could persuade him to do anything, it was too late."

The detective, apologetically. "I reckon maybe I wasn't up on my toes like I ought to've been, Lieutenant, but it sounded kind of screwy to me at first." He addresses Nick, "I didn't know she was *your* wife then."

Nick. "You never can tell where you're going to find one of my wives."

The sound of music suddenly stops. Out in the restaurant, the customers, complaining about this unaccustomed early closing, are being shooed out.

Polly flares up, saying angrily "What are you picking

on Phil for? What's the matter with Robert's wife killing him? He told me himself she was batty as a pet cuckoo and would blow up and gum the whole thing if she found out that this guy—" pointing at David "—was paying him to go away. Maybe she did find out about the bonds. What's the matter with that?"

Abrams looks thoughtfully at David and says, "Hmmm, so that's where the bonds came from?"

Dancer is watching Polly with hard, suspicious eyes. Nick, surprised, asks David, "Bonds?"

David nods slowly.

Abrams says to Polly, "This is no time to stop talking—go on, tell us more about this bond deal."

Caspar comes forward importantly, saying to Polly "No, no, I think this is a very good time to stop talking at least until you've had some sort of legal advice—"

Polly says, "They know about it. Anyway, he does" (indicating David). "Besides, you're Dancer's and Lum's mouthpiece, not mine. How do I know you won't leave me holding the bag?"

Abrams looks pleased for the first time since he's come into the room. He says to Polly, "Now just a minute—that's fine!" He turns to Caspar and says, "So you aren't her lawyer? Well, that'll give us a little rest from your poppin' off. You and your two clients are going outside and wait until we get through talking to the little lady—"

Caspar starts to protest, but Abrams nods to his detectives and two of them take Caspar, Lum Kee, and Dancer out. At the door, Dancer turns to warn Polly. "Don't get yourself in any deeper than you have to."

62

When the door is closed behind him, Abrams sits down with a sigh of relief and says, "It's a lot better in here without them—especially that little shyster. Now maybe we can get somewhere!" He turns and sees that Nick, Nora, and David are huddled together whispering in a far corner of the room. David is telling Nick about Selma and the gun. Abrams says gloomily, "There it is again. If people got anything to say, why don't they say it to me?"

The huddle breaks up, Nick saying "Just a little family gossip."

Abrams says, "I'd even like to hear that." He asks Polly, "Did you ever see Mr. Graham before?"

Polly says, "I saw him tonight, when we went to get the bonds."

Abrams asks, "You and Robert Landis went to get them?"

Polly says, "Yes. He was waiting for us on the corner of ———— Street—and he gave them to Robert."

Abrams asks, "And then what?"

Polly says, "And then nothing. We left him and Robert went home."

Abrams asks, "And what did you do?"

Polly, after a moment's hesitation, says, "I went with him."

Abrams asks, "He took you home with him?"

Polly says, "Well, not in the house. I waited for him a block away—around the corner."

Abrams asks, "And then what?"

Polly says, "I waited a long time and then I heard a shot—only I thought it might be an automobile backfire—it was foggy and I was too far away to see anything—and I didn't know what to do—then after a while a policeman went past the doorway where I was standing—and a police car came—then I honestly didn't know what had happened, but I thought I'd better get out of the neighborhood if I didn't want to get in trouble—so I came back here—"

Abrams says, "Phooey!" and looks at Nick.

Nick says, "I think somebody ought to ask her where she was too far away from—"

Polly stammers, "From wherever it was it happened. If I hadn't been too far away, I'd have known where it was, wouldn't I?"

Nick says, "I give up."

Abrams. "All right—we'll come back to that later. So you were waiting for him? What were you going to do if he hadn't been killed?"

Polly glances uneasily at the door through which Dancer went, then shrugs and says, "We were going away."

Abrams. "Where to?"

Polly. "New York first, I suppose—then Europe, he said."

Abrams (looking at her evening gown). "Dressed like that?"

Polly. "We were going to stop at my place for me to change."

Abrams. "Dancer know you were going?"

Polly. "No."

Abrams. "Think he found it out, and knocked Landis off?"

64

Polly, shaking her head quickly from side to side. "No!"

Abrams. "You're supposed to be Dancer's gal, aren't you?"

Polly. "I work for him."

Abrams. "That's not what I asked you."

Polly. "You've got it wrong—honest. He knew I was running around with Robert—ask anybody."

Abrams. "How long?"

Polly. "A month—three weeks anyhow."

Abrams. "Get much money out of Landis?"

Polly, hesitantly. "He gave me some."

Abrams. "How much?"

Polly. "I don't know exactly. I—I can tell you tomorrow, I guess."

Abrams. "Did you split it with Dancer?"

Polly. "Why, no!"

Abrams. "Maybe you're lying. Maybe Dancer found out you were going away where you could keep all the sugar to yourself—and he put a stopper to it."

Polly. "That's silly!"

Abrams. "Sure. And hanging up in the air with a hunk of rope around your neck is silly, too."

After a little pause to let that sink in, he says, "Landis hadn't been home for a couple of days. Was he with you?"

Polly. "Most of the time."

Abrams. "Drunk?"

Polly. "Yes."

Abrams. "In your apartment?"

Polly. "There and here."

Abrams. "Anybody else with you in your apartment?"

Polly. "No."

Abrams. "Let's get back to the money. How much did you get out of him—roughly?"

Polly stares at the floor in silence.

Abrams. "As much as a grand or two? Or more?"

Polly, not looking up. "More."

Abrams. "More than five grand?" Polly nods. "All right, kick through—about how much?"

Polly shrugs wearily, opens her bag, takes out a check and gives it to Abrams, saying "A couple hundred dollars besides that, I guess."

Abrams looks at the check, then up at the girl and asks, "What'd he give you this for?"

Polly. "Well, I was chucking up a job and everything to go away with him, and I didn't want to take chances on being stranded somewhere off in Europe."

Abrams. "Looks like you didn't, all right." He beckons to the others, who come to look over his shoulders at the check. It is to the order of Polly Byrnes for $10,000 and is signed by Robert Landis. They look at one another in amazement.

Nick says, "Where do you suppose he got hold of that much?"

Abrams. "Why? Aren't they rich?"

Nick. "The money is his wife's, and she found out some time ago that she had to stop giving him too much at a time—just on account of things like this."

Abrams. "Yeah? How about the signature?"

Nick. "Looks all right to me."

66

David. "And to me."

Abrams (as if thinking aloud). "But he don't usually have this much money, huh?" He asks Polly, "Sure you didn't take this to the bank today and find out it was no good?"

Polly. "I did not."

Abrams. "That's something we can check up. You know you're not going to have any easy time collecting this—unless his wife's as big a sap as he was."

Polly. "Why? He gave it to me."

Abrams. "Maybe. But his bank account's automatically tied up now till the estate's settled, and then I got an idea you're going to have to do a fancy piece of suing—taking a drunk for his roll!"

Polly. "I'll take my chances. Just the same, if his dying makes all that trouble, that shows we didn't have anything to do with killing him, doesn't it? Why wouldn't we wait till after we'd cashed it?"

Abrams. "We, we, we! So Dancer *was* in on it! How about the Chinaman?"

Polly. "Nobody was in on it. There was nothing to be in on."

Abrams. "Phooey!" He addresses the remaining detective. "Okay, Butch. Take her and her two playmates down to the Hall and let the district attorney's office know you've got 'em there. We'll be along in a little while." He turns to Nick. "Or do you want to ask her something?"

Nick. "Yes. Did Robert Landis know Pedro Dominges?"

Polly shakes her head and says, "Not that I—" She

remembers something. "Once when Robert and I were
going out together, we passed him and he said good
evening to both of us by name and we couldn't figure
out how he knew Robert's, and Robert made some joke
about nobody being able to hide anything from a landlord."

Nick. "Thanks."

Polly and the detective go out.

Abrams. "That mean anything to you?"

Nick. "Not too much."

Abrams. "Now, Mr. Graham, I've got to—" He
breaks off to look at Nora and Nick, saying thoughtfully "I don't know whether you two ought to be in
here while I'm doing this or not."

Nick, yawning, says, "I know where we ought to be.
Come on, darling."

Abrams. "Maybe you *ought* to stay. Now, Mr.
Graham, I got to ask a lot of questions that you're not
going to like, but I got to ask 'em."

David. "I understand."

Abrams. "First off, you're in love with Mrs. Landis.
Right?" David starts to protest, then simply nods. "She
in love with you?"

David, trying to speak calmly in spite of the painful-
ness of this inquiry. "You'll have to ask her."

Abrams. "I will. Did she ever say she was?"

David. "Not—not since she was married."

Abrams. "Before?"

David. "We were once engaged."

Abrams. "Until Landis came along?"

David, in a very low voice. "Yes."

Abrams. "Ever ask her to divorce him and marry you?"

David. "She knew how I felt—it wasn't necessary to—"

Abrams. "But did you ever ask her?"

David. "I may have."

Abrams. "And what did she say?"

David. "She never said she would."

Abrams. "But you hoped she would. And you thought with him out of the way she would."

David looks Abrams in the eye and says, "I didn't kill Robert."

Abrams. "I said you did? But you did pay him to go away."

David. "Yes."

Abrams. "Did she know about it?"

David. "No, not unless he told her."

Abrams. "Were you and Landis on good terms?"

David. "Decidedly not."

Abrams. "On very bad terms?"

David. "Very bad."

The lights go out. In complete darkness Abrams' voice is heard saying "Stay where you are—everybody!"

From the distance come the sounds of doors crashing, of glass breaking, of feet running, of men shouting; then close at hand furniture is knocked over, a door is slammed open, feet pound on the floor, two shots are fired, bodies thud and thrash around on the floor. Presently a cigarette lighter snaps on, held in Nick's hand. Behind him, in the dim light, Nora's and David's faces can be seen. The three of them are looking down at their feet. Abrams lies on the floor on his back. On top of him, mechanically chewing gum, his face serene, is Harold. One of his feet is on Abrams' throat; both his hands are clamped around one of Abrams' feet, twisting it inward and upward in the old Gotch toe-hold.

Nick says gently, "Harold, Harold, get up from there. Lieutenant Abrams isn't going to like this."

Harold, cheerfully. "You're the boss." He jumps up.

As Abrams gets up, a hand to his throat, Nick says, "My chauffeur. Stout fellow, eh?"

Abrams goes toward Harold, saying "What do you think you—"

Harold sticks his face into the lieutenant's and says, "What am I supposed to do? I'm sitting out there and I see the lights go off. Nick and Mrs. Charles are up here and I know what kind of dump it is. Think I'm going to sit out there like a sissy till they throw the bodies out? How do I know you're a copper?" Then more argumentatively as he goes on. "Suppose I did know it? How can I tell Nick ain't got hisself in a jam with the police?"

Nick. "All right—but don't you boys think you'd better stop wrangling long enough to find out who turned out the lights and did the shooting?" He asks Harold, "Did you run into anybody else on your way up?"

Harold. "Only the copper, here."

The lights go on.

They are standing in the passageway outside Dancer's apartment. As they start toward the front of the building, out of the restaurant comes one of Abrams' men with Polly, Lum Kee, and Caspar, and behind them another detective, dragging a Chinese waiter.

Abrams asks in a complaining voice, "Well, now what have you been letting them do?"

One of the detectives, indicating the waiter, says, "Dancer had this monkey pull the switch and beat it out a window. Butch is hunting for him now."

Abrams asks, "And what was that shooting?"

The other detective says sheepishly, "I guess it was me. I thought there was somebody running at me but I guess it was only me in the mirror."

Abrams says wearily, "All right—but this time take them down to the Hall like I told you."

David has taken Nick a little aside and is asking "Should I tell him about Selma and the gun?"

Nick. "It depends on whether you think she did it."

David. "Of course not—do you?"

Nick. "No. Then the only thing to do is to tell him everything."

At this point, Abrams, returning from seeing his men off, says, "I asked you people not to go off whispering in corners all the time."

David. "Lieutenant Abrams, I've something to tell you. I happened..."

Abrams interrupts him. "All right—but we're all going down to the Hall where we can talk in peace. I don't like the high jinks that come off here."

Nora yawns.

Abrams. "Sorry, Mrs. Charles. I won't keep you any longer than I have to but we've got to do things regular."

A cheap hotel room. Phil is sitting at a table playing solitaire with a gun on the table. He is smoking nervously and there is a pile of cigarette butts on a saucer near him. Presently there is a knock on the door. He picks up the gun and stares at the door with frightened eyes but doesn't answer. The knock is repeated, louder. After a little pause, Dancer's voice comes through, saying "This is Dancer—will you open the door or will I kick it in?"

Slowly, as if afraid to open the door and afraid not to, Phil gets up and, holding the gun behind him, goes to the door and unlocks it. Dancer pushes the door open violently, knocking Phil back against the wall, then kicks the door shut; and standing close to Phil, says with threatening mildness, "What did I tell you about trying to cut yourself in on somebody else's game?"

Outside the Hall of Justice—broad daylight. Harold is asleep in Nick's car. Nick, Nora, and Abrams come out of the building surrounded by a flock of reporters.

Abrams is saying to the reporters "Lay off us. I told you anything you get, you'll have to get from the DA." He then says to Nick and Nora, "I could use a lot of breakfast. How about you folks?"

Nick looks at his watch and says, "I could use a lot of sleep."

Nora is too sleepy to say anything.

Abrams insists. "Yeah, but you got to eat anyhow, don't you, and there's a pretty good place not far from here."

Nick asks, "You mean you want to ask some more questions?"

Abrams. "No, not exactly, but there are a couple of points."

Nick. "We'll drop you wherever you're going and you can ask them on the way—but if you get wrong answers it's because I'm talking in my sleep."

As they are about to get into Nick's car, a taxicab drives up and Dancer gets out. Abrams goes over and grabs him by the shoulder, asking "Where have you been?"

Dancer. "Hiding—where'd you think I've been? The lights go out and somebody starts shooting—I haven't even got a gun—I don't know whether somebody's trying to get me or if I'm being framed by you people, or what—so I did the only smart thing I could think of and played the duck and waited for daylight so I can at least see who's shooting at me."

Abrams turns to Nick and says, "Phooey! I won't be more than a minute. I'm going to turn him over to the boys. I'm afraid to trust myself with him this morning—I'm liable to slap him around too much." He and Dancer go back into the Hall of Justice.

Abrams returns almost immediately, gets into the car with Nick and Nora complaining "What stories these guys think up." They drive off.

———

73

Interior Nick's car. Nick, Nora, and Abrams are sitting together. Nora is nodding sleepily, her head keeps bobbing in front of Nick, interfering with his vision. Whenever Nick turns to speak to Abrams, her head falls back, concealing him.

Abrams. "Sure I believe David Graham—I guess, but how do I know he ought to have believed Mrs. Landis? Well, I'm going to talk to her today, if I have to lock up that lame nut doctor while I do it. On the level, Mr. Charles. What's she doing with him around if she isn't at least a little bit punchy?"

Nick. "I don't think she is—just very nervous. You know how idle wives get—look at Mrs. Charles, for instance."

Abrams looks at Nora, who by this time is sound asleep, her chin resting on her chest.

Nick goes on—"and then, living with Robert wasn't doing her any good."

Abrams. "You honestly don't think she did it?"
Nick. "No."

Abrams. "She had the best reason. Graham had paid him to go away and he was going away, so *he* didn't have much reason—Dancer and the Chinaman and the Byrnes gal were taking him all right, but killing him made it tough for them on the check. Besides, why didn't they grab the bonds and that jewelry of his wife's that he had on him? And that goes for the Byrnes gal, even if she was double-crossing the others."

Nick asks, "How about Phil—her brother?"

Abrams. "There's no telling exactly until we get hold of him, but he figures to be out for the dough, too—so

74

why don't he grab the bonds? He don't sound to me like a lad who would kill somebody just because he was running off with his sister."

Nick. "Lots of stickups go wrong—perhaps he had to leave before he could get the stuff."

Abrams. "You mean on account of Mrs. Landis running around the corner with a gun in her hand like she said she did? If he saw her, why didn't she see him, and she didn't say anything about that, did she?"

Nick. "Back in the office, you said Landis and Pedro were killed with bullets from the same gun. She doesn't fit in very well with Pedro's killing; but Polly lived in his house, which ties his killing up at least a little with her and the others."

Abrams. "That's right enough, and I guess there's not much doubt that he was killed because he was on his way to tell you something. It's a fair bet that that something he was going to tell you had to do with Robert Landis, but there's something funny about that house that I want to show you. Maybe, if you've got a few minutes—"

Nick. "You don't mean the goats in the hallway?"

Abrams, surprised. "What goats?"

Nick. "Never mind—but Mr. and Mrs. Charles aren't going anywhere but home—to sleep. Think you'll be able to fish Mrs. Landis' gun up from where David threw it?"

Abrams. "I guess so. Anyway, the boys are down there working now." He pauses. "—and when we get that, then we'll know. It will only take a few minutes to go over to that apartment house."

Nick. "Call me later. We've been on a train for three days and look what kind of a night we've had."

Abrams. "All right—I could use a little sleep myself but I've got to talk to Mrs. Landis and got to stop at the bank and see about that check."

Harold pulls over to the curb and Abrams gets out. Nora almost falls out after him as he withdraws his support. Abrams helps Nick put her back on the seat and placing her head on his shoulder, Nick nods good-bye to Abrams, who waves to him as they drive off.

Nick and Nora in their car going home. She is sleeping on his shoulder. With his free hand he unties his neck-tie and takes off his shirt. When he twists around a little to unbutton his collar, in back, Nora wakes up and asks, "What are you doing?"

Nick. "I'm getting as few clothes as possible between me and bed."

Nora. "That's cheating." She begins to loosen her clothes. They arrive at the house. As they go up the front steps, Nora says, "Last one in bed is a sissy!" They run into the house pulling off clothes.

From the living room to meet them come Asta and the reporters that they left at the Hall of Justice, the reporters asking questions "Do the police suspect Mrs. Landis?" "What connections had Pedro Dominges with the Landis killing?" et cetera, et cetera.

Nick insists he knows nothing about it and has nothing to say as they go back into the living room, winding up with "I'm going to give you boys one drink apiece and then put you out."

One of the reporters asks, "Well, answer another question for us and we won't print it if you don't want us to. Is it true that you actually didn't retire as a detective but are working under cover?"

Nick, starting to pour drinks. "No, it's not true, but don't print it because I don't want my wife's relatives to know I'm living on her money."

A stone with a piece of paper wrapped around it crashes through the glass of the window and knocks the bottle out of his hand. Asta joyfully grabs the stone, runs under a sofa with it, and starts to chew the paper off while Nick and the reporters scramble after him. By the time Nick recovers the stone with the paper, the note has been pretty well chewed up. He spreads it out, glances at it and puts it in his pocket before the reporters, who are crowding around him, can read it.

Nick. "Silly little woman. I told her to stop writing me."

The reporters, failing to get anything else out of Nick, rush out to see if they can find out who threw the stone. Nick smooths the note out and he and Nora, patching it as well as they can where Asta's teeth have torn it, read it. It is crudely printed.

MR. CHARLS PHIL BYRNES ALIAS RALPH WEST IS A EX CON AND WAS MARRIED TO POLLY IN TOPEKER THREE YERS AGO. HE LIVES AT THE MIL

The rest of the note has been chewed off by Asta.

Nick, indifferently. "Well, what are we supposed to do, send them an anniversary present?"

Nora. "Nick, phone Lieutenant Abrams!"

Nick. "And have him up here to keep us awake some more?"

Nora insists. "Phone him, Nick. Don't you see, if Phil was her husband . . ."

Nick grumbles, "I guess you're right," and goes out of the room.

Nora plays with Asta for a minute or two and then goes to the door of the next room where the phone is. Not seeing Nick, she calls him. There is no answer. After a little hesitancy, she goes up to the bedroom. Nick, in pajamas, is asleep. On her pillow is a sign: SISSY.

Aunt Katherine at telephone at her home. Dr. Kammer is sitting in a chair nearby. She calls a number and asks, "Mr. Moody. This is Miss Forrest calling."

Series of Short Shots. Printing press running off extras with enormous headlines: MEMBER OF PROMINENT FAMILY KILLED.

Editorial room of newspaper office—men being assigned to cover this story.

Then up to publisher's office, where Peter Moody, a very dignified old man with a grave and courteous manner, is picking up the phone, saying "Yes, Katherine, how are you? I'm awfully sorry to hear about Robert's death."

Aunt Katherine. "Thank you, Peter. It's terrible

and that's what I called you about. The police, it seems, are trying to make a great deal of mystery out of what must have been—it couldn't have been anything else—simply an attempted holdup. I hope I can count on you to do your best to give the whole terrible affair no more publicity than is absolutely necessary."

Peter Moody. "Of course, of course, Katherine. But you must understand that if the police make it news we must print it."

Aunt Katherine. "I understand, but you will handle it as quietly as possible?"

Moody. "Certainly, I can promise you that. And will you please convey my sympathy to poor Selma."

Aunt Katherine. "Thank you, Peter."

As Peter Moody puts down the phone, a man comes into the office bringing an early copy of the extra that had been run off with the enormous headline seen in the previous shot.

Moody looks at it and nods with approval, saying "Very good."

Aunt Katherine phones her brother, the general, who is having his whiskers trimmed by a valet almost as old as he is. The valet hands him the phone, saying "Miss Forrest, sir."

The general hems and haws between his words a good deal. "It's terrible, Katherine—I just heard—I'm on my way over."

Aunt Katherine. "Yes, terrible, Thomas and I want to see you—but first, will you see if you can get in touch with the mayor?"

General. "The mayor?" He clears his throat some more.

Aunt Katherine. "Yes. I'm sure poor Robert was killed by a robber, but the police seem determined to make as big a mystery out of it, with as much resultant notoriety for all of us as possible. I wish you would ask him to do what he can."

General. "Certainly, my dear," clearing his throat again, "I shall look after it immediately."

As Katherine hangs up, he gives the valet the phone, saying "Get me the mayor" in the tone one says, "Get me a newspaper."

As Aunt Katherine turns from the phone toward Dr. Kammer, the butler appears at the door to announce Lieutenant Abrams.

Several hours later, the general arrives at Nick's house. He hands his hat to the butler who opens the door and says, "Take me to Mr. Charles immediately."

Butler. "But he's still asleep, sir."

The general snorts, saying "Yes, yes, so you said when Miss Forrest phoned. Devilish inconsiderate of all of you."

The butler says apologetically, "But we never disturb him when he's asleep, sir."

The general snorts some more. "You said that over the phone, too. Now stop this silly nonsense and take me to him."

The butler, overawed by the general, takes him up to Nick and Nora's room. They are sleeping soundly.

The general prods one of Nora's shoulders with his finger and says, "Here, here, wake up."

Nora stirs a little and mumbles something but doesn't open her eyes.

The general prods her again, saying "Come—this is no time to be sleeping. Devilish inconsiderate of all of you."

This time Nora opens her eyes and stares up at him in amazement.

General. "Wake up your young man, my dear. Why doesn't the fellow sleep at night?"

Nora asks, "But what's the matter, Uncle Thomas?"

General. "Matter? We've been trying to get you for hours. Wake him up."

Nora shakes Nick, who says without opening his eyes, "Go away porter, I told you not to call me till Sacramento."

Nora. "Wake up, Nick, Uncle Thomas wants to talk to you."

Nick. "Tell the white-whiskered old fossil to do his snorting in somebody else's ear—I'm busy."

Nora. "But Nick, he's here, standing beside you."

Nick sits up blinking and says, "Why, Uncle Thomas, how nice of you to drop in on us like this."

General. "Come—enough of this nonsense. Selma has been arrested and you lie here snoring."

Nora looks horrified.

The general snorts some more. "The mayor did nothing to stop it—the bounder."

Nick. "Maybe he didn't know."

The general asks, "Didn't know what?"

Nick. "That I was snoring."

General. "Come, get up. You know about these things—Katherine is counting on you."

Nick, putting on his robe and slippers, says, "You don't need me now, you need a lawyer."

The general says contemptuously, "A lawyer—old Witherington is running around in circles, completely at sea; no ability at all, that fellow."

Nick. "Then why don't you get another lawyer?"

The general draws himself up. "Witherington has been our family attorney for years."

Nick. "Well, what do you expect me to do?"

General. "To make the police stop being so silly—to get Selma out of there right away—to put an end to all this beastly notoriety."

Nick asks, "Is that all?"

General. "Come—we're wasting time—get into your clothes."

In a barely furnished office in the Hall of Justice, Nick is talking to Abrams.

Abrams. "I know how you feel about it, Mr. Charles, I guess I'd feel the same way if it was one of my family; but what can we do? Everything points to her."

Nick asks, "You mean you found out some things I don't know about?"

Abrams. "Well, not much, maybe, but there's that check thing."

Nick asks, "What check thing?"

Abrams. "Maybe the district attorney isn't going to like this much, but I'll tell you: I went down to Landis' bank and that ten-thousand-dollar check he gave the girl is perfectly okay. It was okay because his wife had put ten thousand in there for him just the day before."

Nick looks surprised. He asks, "Are you sure?"

Abrams. "Sure, I'm sure. I saw it myself."

Nick. "Did you ask her about it?"

Abrams replies wearily, "Yes, and there's some kind of hanky-panky there, too, but I can't figure out just what it is. She started to say she didn't and then the old lady, Miss Katherine," he breaks off to add—"that one's a holy terror—"

Nick. "Make two copies of that."

Abrams. "—she spoke up and said, 'You did, Selma, you told me so yourself,' and then Mrs. Landis said yes, she did."

Nick asks, "So where does that fit in?"

Abrams. "So maybe she gave it to him and found out he was passing it on to the girl—how do I know? Every time I tried to pin her down she gets hysterical."

Nick asks, "Find out anything else at the bank?"

Abrams. "No. He had given the Byrnes gal a check for a hundred dollars and one for seventy-five, like she told us." He takes the checks out of a desk drawer, saying "Here, if you want to see them."

Nick looks at them and asks, "Have you got the ten-thousand-dollar check he gave her?"

Abrams. "Yes." He gives it to him.

Nick stands up, tilting back a light-shade, holds one of the small checks with the $10,000 check over it up against the light and tries the big check with the other small one. Abrams stands up to look over his shoulder.

Nick fiddles with the checks until the signature of the top one is exactly over the bottom one.

Abrams exclaims, "A forgery!"

Nick nods, saying "Yes, a tracing. Nobody ever writes *that* much the same twice."

Abrams picks up the telephone and says, "Give me Joe," then says, "Joe, go out and pick up that Polly Byrnes for me."

When he puts down the phone, Nick asks, "You aren't holding any of them?"

Abrams shakes his head and says, "No. The guns we got from the Chinaman and Dancer are .38's all right, like he was killed with, but the experts say they are not the guns that did it. I'm still not too sure this forgery is going to help Mrs. Landis much. I already told you I knew there was some hanky-panky about these checks."

Nick asks, "You haven't found her gun yet?"

Abrams. "I got a couple of men in diving suits working over the bottom down around where David Graham threw it. But it was night, you know, and we can't be too sure of the exact spot."

Nick. "And you think you are going to convict her if you don't find the gun?"

Abrams. "Maybe I do and maybe I don't. It's what the district attorney thinks."

Nick. "Does he think she killed Pedro Dominges?"

Abrams. "That's not funny, Mr. Charles. Her alibi covering that time is just no good at all. She claims a compact had been mailed to her from the Li-Chee and she sent it back saying it wasn't hers; but she thinks it belongs to some woman who was there with Robert, so that afternoon, when she's kind of nuts over him not being home for a couple of days, she goes down there to see if she can find out about him. Of course that joint don't open till evening and so she didn't see anybody that could tell us she was there. She says she went back home again and that just about covers the time that Dominges was being killed. On the level, Mr. Charles, we had nobody else but her that we could hold."

Nick. "Found your Selma Young yet?"

Abrams. "No."

Nick. "How about Phil?"

Abrams. "Sure, maybe, if we can find him."

Nick takes out the note that was thrown through the window, gives it to Abrams.

Abrams reads it carefully, then asks, "And where did this come from?"

Nick. "Somebody wrapped it around a dornick and heaved it through my window."

Abrams asks, "Where's the rest of it?"

Nick. "Somewhere in my dog's intestines."

Abrams reads slowly, "—lives at the Mil———"

Nick pushes the telephone book over to him and says, "Maybe that won't be so tough. Polly said he lived in a hotel on Turk Street."

Abrams. "That's right." He opens the telephone book to the "hotel" classification and runs his finger down the "Mi" entries, finally coming to the Miltern Hotel,—Turk Street.

Abrams. "That could be it—want to give it a try with me?"

Nick. "Right!" They get up. As they go toward the door, Nick says, "You noticed that whoever wrote the note misspelled easy words like my name and 'years,' but did all right with 'alias' and 'married'?"

Abrams. "Yeah, I noticed."

Exterior of Miltern Hotel—a small, shabby, dirty joint with a door between two stores, and stairs leading up to an office on the second floor. Abrams, Nick, and two other detectives get out of a car which draws up with no sound of sirens. One of the men remains at the outer door. Nick, Abrams, and the other detective start up the stairs. They go up to a small and dark office. Nobody is there. Abrams knocks on the battered counter. After a little while, a man in dirty shirt-sleeves appears. Abrams asks him, "Is Mr. Phil Byrnes in?"

The man says, "We ain't got no Mr. Byrnes—not even a Mrs. Byrnes."

Abrams. "Have you got a Ralph West?"

The man. "Yep."

Abrams. "Is he in?"

The man. "I don't know—room 212—next floor."

Abrams says to the detective with him, "Get on the back stairs."

Abrams and Nick walk up the front stairs and down a dark hall until they find room 212. Abrams knocks on the door—there is no answer. He knocks again, saying in what he tries to make a youthful voice "Telegram for Mr. West." There is still no answer. He looks at Nick. Nick reaches past him and turns the knob, pushing the door open.

Nick. "After you, my dear Lieutenant."

Sprawled on his back across the bed, very obviously dead, is Phil, fully dressed as when we last saw him.

Nick points to something on the floor between them and the bed. It is a pair of spectacles, the frame bent, the glass ground almost to a powder. Abrams nods and comes into the room, stepping over the glasses, and leans over Phil.

Abrams. "Dead, all right—strangled, and he was beaten up some before the strangling set in." He looks down at one of Phil's hands, then picks it up and takes half a dozen hairs from it. Turning to show them to Nick, he says, "Somebody's hair in his hand."

Nick looks at the hairs, then at the broken glasses on the floor. He says nothing. It is obvious he is trying to figure something out.

Abrams goes out saying "Wait a minute—I'll have one of the boys phone and then we'll give the room a good casing."

Nick moves around the room looking at things, opening and shutting drawers and looking into a closet, but apparently not finding anything of interest until he sees an automatic on the floor under one corner of the bed. He bends down to look at it but doesn't touch it.

While Nick is looking at the gun, Abrams returns to the room.

Nick. "Here's another .38 for your experts to match up."

Abrams. "Hmm, what do you think?"

Nick. "I don't think—I used to be a detective myself."

Abrams. "Nobody downstairs seems to know about any visitors, but I guess the kind he had wouldn't have gone to the trouble of knocking on the counter like we did."

He leans over Phil and begins to go through his pockets. Then he straightens up and says, "I guess the heater's his. He's wearing an empty shoulder holster." He holds up a flat key and adds, "And I guess this is the key to the Byrnes gal's apartment. It's got her number stamped on it."

Nick. "Another good guess would be that Selma Landis didn't do this."

Abrams: "Fair enough, but he wasn't killed the way the other ones were, either."

Policemen enter, some in plain clothes, some in uniform, and Abrams starts to give them instructions about searching the room, looking for fingerprints, questioning the occupants of adjoining rooms, et cetera, et cetera.

Nick. "And I think you ought to have your laboratory look at that hair and the cheaters," indicating the broken glasses.

Abrams. "Okay." He looks curiously at Nick.

Nick. "And the sooner, the better."

Abrams, again. "Okay." He addresses one of the men standing and listening to them. "Do it." He hands him the hair. Then turning back to Nick, he says, "Anything particular on your mind?"

Nick. "Ought to be on yours, with three murders tied together in just about twenty-four hours. Now that we've been told he's her husband and he's dead, don't you think we ought to see Polly as soon as possible?"

Abrams says, "There's something in that" and tells one of his men, "Don't let these lugs dog it while I'm gone." He and Nick go downstairs. In the office he uses the telephone. When he's through, he grumbles, "They haven't picked her up yet." He scratches his chin, then says, "I've got a man waiting up in her apartment. Want to take a run up there? I told you there's something funny about the place that I'd like you to see."

Nick. "All right. Don't you think now we've got something more to talk about to Dancer?"

Abrams says in a hurt tone, "I think of things sometimes. I told them to pick up him and the Chinaman both."

They go downstairs to the street.

At Aunt Katherine's, all the Forrests except Selma are assembled. They are very excited and keep moving around so that Asta, who obviously doesn't like any of them, has a great deal of difficulty keeping out of their way. Nora and Dr. Kammer are also there.

The general is standing, glaring down at Nora, and asking indignantly, "Do you mean to say that this— ah—husband of yours actually advised David to tell the police about Selma and the pistol?"

Nora says defiantly, "Yes."

The general starts to walk up and down the floor, sending Asta into hiding again, and rumpling his whiskers and growling. "Why, the fellow's a scoundrel —an out-and-out scoundrel."

Nora. "Nick's not—he knows what he's doing."

The general snorts and says angrily, "Nonsense—nobody knows what they're doing. The whole country is full of incompetents and scoundrels nowadays."

Aunt Hattie nudges Aunt Lucy and asks, "What is Thomas saying now—he mutters so."

Aunt Lucy, who has been sniffling into her handkerchief, sobs, "Poor Selma. This is a terrible thing to happen to me—only a week after my eighty-third birthday."

Nora jumps up and says, "Nick's not incompetent and he's not a scoundrel. You're all acting as if you thought Selma really killed Robert."

Aunt Katherine and Dr. Kammer exchange significant glances. The general clears his throat and says, "It's not a case of anybody killing anybody—it's a case of his being so devilish inconsiderate of the family. Has the fellow no feelings?"

William, who is considered not too bright by the family, runs his finger inside his too-tight collar and asks, "Does anyone know if the police have considered the theory that Robert might have committed suicide?"

Aunt Katherine snaps at him, "That will do, William," while the rest of them glare at him.

Burton, his tic working overtime, asks, "Well, where is this Nicholas? Why isn't he here to explain himself?"

Nora. "Because he's out trying to clear Selma while you all sit around here and criticize him."

The general says, "I'd never have asked him if I'd known what the fellow'd been up to."

Nora rises with great dignity and calls Asta. She

faces the family and says, "I'm sure he doesn't care what any of you think—he's not doing it for you—he's doing it for Selma. Good-bye."

What would otherwise have been a dignified exit is spoiled by her bumping into the antique butler as she goes through the door. After the butler has gotten his breath, he says, "Mr. Graham on the phone for you, Mrs. Charles."

She goes to the phone and says, "Hello, David."

David, at the other end of the wire, asks excitedly, "Where is Nick? I tried your house and the detective bureau but he wasn't there. Lieutenant Abrams wasn't in either."

Nora. "They're probably out together. Oh, Lieutenant Abrams said something about wanting Nick to go over to that apartment house with him. Maybe they're there. What is it, David?"

David. "Something's happened—I've got to see Nick. What apartment house?"

Nora. "I'm leaving here now. I'll meet you and take you there. Where are you?"

David. "I'm in a drugstore at Mason and Bush streets."

Nora. "Wait for me—I'll be right over."

They hang up and she, after making a face at the direction of the room where she left the family, goes out and gets into her car.

Abrams and Nick arrive at the building where Polly has an apartment. It is a large, shabby building, set at the foot of Telegraph Hill. Across the street from it the hill rises steep and unpaved, with winding, wooden steps leading up between scattered small frame houses. The end of the street, even with the house's left-hand wall, is closed by a high board fence. From the fence, as from the house wall, the ground falls perpendicularly fifty or sixty feet to a rock-strewn vacant lot covering several blocks. In the street and on the hill above, goats are roaming. As they approach the door a goat runs out and dodges past them and goes to join the others. The front door is open. Abrams and Nick go in. Abrams knocks on a door on the left side of the corridor. The door is opened by a plainclothesman who says, "Nary hide or hair of her yet."

A policeman in uniform and another in plain clothes are bent over a table doing a crossword puzzle together. They rise hastily as Abrams comes in, but he pays no attention to them.

Abrams, as they go in. "This is Polly's apartment. There's nothing much here except you'll notice the rug's new."

Nick looks at the rug and says, "Oh, I saw a new one once in a store window."

Abrams, patiently. "All right, but wait—maybe it don't mean anything, maybe it does."

Nick asks, "What do you think it means?"

Abrams sighs and says, "If I knew, do you think I'd be wasting your time dragging you up here? We'll go back here, now." He leads the way out of Polly's apartment down the hall to an apartment on the same floor in the rear, unlocking it with a key from his pocket, saying as he opens the door "This is the fellow's that was killed—that Pedro Dominges."

Nick says quickly, "Another new rug—I said it first."

Abrams, pointing to the other end of the living room, where there is a rug rolled up and lying against the wall. "There's another one."

Nick asks, "What is this rug racket? Are we hunting for an Armenian?"

Abrams. "Maybe you're right in kidding me—maybe none of this means anything, but just the same, he bought twelve rugs only a couple of days ago and that's just how many apartments he's got in the place." He walks over to the table and says, "Here's the bill. And the one apartment that didn't get a rug was rented only last week to somebody named Anderson. No front name—no Mr. or Miss or Mrs., according to his books here. I want to show you that next."

Nick asks, "What have you found out about him?"

Abrams. "Nothing. This guy Dominges ran this place by himself. We haven't found anybody who ever saw this Anderson."

There is a terrific uproar from the corridor. They go to the door to see Asta, a goat, and Nora (at the other end of Asta's leash) all tangled up together, while David is trying to untangle them. When the goat has finally been chased out, they all return to Pedro's apartment.

As Nick helps Nora brush off her clothes, she says, "Why that drunken man was right—there *are* goats in the hall."

Nick. "You can always trust my friends, drunk or sober. Is that what you came down here to find out?"

Nora. "No. David has something to show you."

David takes from his pocket a sheet of paper, on which in the same crude printing as on Nick's note is:

93

IF YOU WANT TO SAFE THAT DISSY
DAME OF YOURN YOU BETER MAKE
DANCER TELL HOW HE FOWND OUT
LAST NIGHT PHIL BYRNES WAS
POLLY'S HUSBIND
                    A FRIEND

After they have read it, Abrams asks, "How'd it
come to you?"

David. "It was under my door when I woke up
today."

Nick. "The same half-smart attempt at illiteracy as
the one I got."

Abrams. "Yeah—but that don't have to mean that
what it says is wrong. Running out yours got us something, so why don't we run out this?"

Nick. "We'll have to wait until you pick up your
people. Now how about this Anderson?"

Abrams. "To tell you the truth, Mr. Charles, I don't
believe there ever was any Anderson, but you can—"

Nick. "Tut-tut—don't be so skeptical; you read his
fairy tales when you were a child."

Abrams, patiently. "Okay, kid me—but what I mean
is—I don't believe *this* Anderson ever was, and I'll
show you why when we get upstairs. As a matter of
fact, I don't believe anybody took that apartment."

Nora. "I took that."

They look at her in surprise. She has gotten up from
the chair and has gone over to an enlarged snapshot
hanging on the wall.

Abrams. "You did what, Mrs. Charles?"

94

Nora. "I took that picture. They're the servants we had at Ross. There's Pedro," she points them out, "Ella, Ann, et cetera."

Pedro looks much as Nora remembered him, except that he is six years younger and his mustache, while not small, is definitely not long, nor is it as white as it was when we saw him.

They all get up to look.

Nick asks, "You're sure that place you had wasn't on Coney Island?" He turns to Abrams and says, "I apologize for the domestic comedy. Let's go up and look at the apartment that you say wasn't rented by a fellow whose name wasn't Anderson."

Abrams leads the way up to the next floor, unlocks the door, leading them into the apartment over Polly's, saying to Nick "See the rug—" The rug is stained and very worn.

Nick. "I get it—it's *not* a new rug."

Abrams. "Yeh, that's one of the things I meant. I've got something else to show you—" He points to a corner of the room where there is a pile of old and battered iron pipe. "But the chief things that we found was that Pedro had the lock changed on the door only yesterday and all the fingerprints we found in here are his."

Nick walks to a window, raises it and looks down the side of the cliff. He says, "A nice drop from here. Would I be guessing wrong if I said that this apartment was right over Polly's?"

Abrams. "No, I guess not."

Nick asks, "Well?"

Abrams. "I don't know, Mr. Charles, for a fact, but not putting a new rug in and only his fingerprints here makes it look to me like he was kind of using the place and not figuring on renting it."

Nick asks, "And you think he changed the lock so he couldn't get in again to keep tenants out?"

Abrams, patiently, as usual, says, "I told you there was something funny here. I told you I didn't know what it was all about."

Nick. "Pedro was killed first. What are you picking on him for?"

Abrams. "What do I know from nothing? If you can think of anything, play your string out."

Nick. "No hard feelings. Don't take me too seriously. Suppose you were going to put a rug down, what would you do first?"

Abrams. "I don't know—I guess I'd get somebody to lug it upstairs."

Nick. "Swell. And then what?"

Abrams. "Then you start at one end of the room and roll it across the floor."

Nick asks, "On top of this one?"

Abrams scratches his head and says, "No, I guess not."

Nick. "All right—let's take this one up first, then."

Abrams. "Okay. You take that corner and I'll take this one."

Nick. "Who, me? Haven't you got hired men down-stairs?"

Abrams. "Sure." He goes outside the door and yells, "Hey, Francis—you and that other cutie who was trying to find a three-letter word for ape, come up here."

96

Nora, in a hoarse whisper, asks, "What is it, Nick?"

Nick "Do I know? Men are dying all around and you ask me riddles."

There is a clumping on the stairs and the plain-clothesman and the uniformed policeman who were working on the crossword puzzle come in.

Abrams says to them, "You boys roll this three-letter word meaning rug down to the other end of a four-letter word meaning 'room.'"

They say "sure" very eagerly, push furniture out of the way and start to roll the rug up. They roll it halfway when Nick says, "Maybe that'll do for the time." He walks over to a spot they have uncovered where six floorboards have been cut across in two places to make about a square foot. "Let's look at this."

Abrams, followed by his two men, goes to the spot Nick has indicated. Abrams opens a pocket knife, puts the blade in, and the sawed boards come up in a section, leaving a square-foot hole. He looks down, then puts his hand in and brings up a pair of flat earpieces on a steel band such as telephone operators wear, attached to a wire running down into the hole.

Nick. "I suppose we know what this is. Send one of the boys downstairs to recite the alphabet in Polly's place."

Abrams jerks a thumb at the plainclothesman and says, "Go ahead, Francis."

Francis goes out. Presently, from down below through the earpieces comes Francis' voice. "A B C D E—" A moment of hesitation, then: "A B C D—"

Nick. "Okay for sound. It was for listening in, all right."

97

Abrams. "Yeah, that's that. What do you guess this Pedro was up to?"

(All through this scene, Asta shows that he is very fond of David, ignoring both Nick and Nora in favor of him.)

Nick. "Well, there's still this junk to figure—" He turns toward the pile of iron pipe in the corner. Asta is busy chewing it. "Get away from the evidence, Asta."

Abrams. "He won't be hurting it much—there was only Pedro's fingerprints on it. What do you guess it was for? I couldn't be thinking anybody would pipe gas through it."

Nick. "Why not? With a layout like this, you can pipe gas in several directions at once." He sits down on the floor and begins to screw sections of the pipe together. (This is actually a ladder, but he keeps the rungs sticking out in all directions and keeps it from being recognizable until, suddenly, when he puts the last piece on and turns it around.)

Nick, holding the finished ladder up, says, "Fifty will get you two-fifty that it will just about reach to Polly's window below, with this piece left over—" picking up an extra part from the floor, "for good measure when he got there."

He takes the ladder to the window, lowers it and hangs it on the sill. It reaches exactly to the sill of Polly's apartment below.

Abrams. "What do you guess he wanted to do that for?"

Francis sticks his head in the door and says, "We

98

got Byrnes. Do you want her up? And we got Dancer and Lum Kee, too."

Abrams looks at Nick and asks, "Will they clutter it up for you? Do you think you got as much out of this place as you want?"

Nick. "The more the merrier. Perhaps not as much as I want, but as much as I think I'm going to get."

Abrams says to Francis, "Okay, feed them to us."

Nick asks Abrams, "What kind of clothes did you find in the place?"

Abrams. "None—not a stitch. Nothing to show anybody ever lived here. That's why I told you I don't believe anybody ever did."

Nick asks, "Where does that fit in? Do you think Pedro was using the place himself—spying on the people downstairs? He's killed first and, half a day later, Robert Landis, who visits downstairs, is killed, and the next day, the brother or husband or something of the gal he visits is killed. How are you going to blame all that on Pedro?"

Abrams, wearily. "Mr. Charles, how many times have I told you there was something funny here I don't understand; and some hanky-panky about the checks I don't understand? Did I ever pretend I knew what all this led to?"

Nick. "Oh, yes—about the checks. We've got to ask these people about them when they come upstairs and maybe they won't want to say right out. What would be wrong with getting Mrs. Landis over so we'd have her here to chuck at them if they think we're fooling?"

Abrams. "I don't know, the DA's kind of—"

Nick. "What—with a police escort?"

Abrams. "Okay—I'll send for her."

Nick. "God will reward you."

Three policemen, one in uniform, bring in Polly, Dancer, and Lum Kee.

Abrams. "Francis, phone the Hall and tell them to bring up Mrs. Landis."

Francis goes to the phone.

Nick, aside to Abrams. "Maybe they don't know. Throw it hard enough to bounce."

Abrams says to Nick, "Okay." Turns to Polly: "Your husband was killed this afternoon. What do you know about it?"

Polly. "I—what?"

Abrams, to Dancer. "Her husband was killed this afternoon."

Dancer. "Her what?"

Abrams. "Cut it out! We're not playing charades."

They look at him blankly.

Abrams, counting out syllables on his fingers, says, "Pol-ly had a hus-band named Phil e-ven if he was sup-posed to be her bro-ther and he was found dead on Turk Street this af-ter-noon."

Polly and Dancer turn to face each other at the same moment, exclaiming simultaneously, "You—!!!" and then breaking off as they realize each is saying the same thing.

Abrams. "You—*you*—you what?"

Neither of them says anything.

Nick says to Abrams, "Simple enough— she started

to accuse *him* of killing Phil because he found out he was her husband and he started to accuse *her* of double-crossing him by not telling him Phil was her husband."

Abrams says to Polly, "He was your husband, wasn't he? Married three years ago in Topeka?"

She nods, glancing sidewise at Dancer. "But I didn't want to have any more to do with him and so when he showed up last week I didn't say anything about it."

Abrams. "What did he go to the pen for?"

Polly. "Blackmail."

Abrams. "And what did he have on you that he was hanging around shaking you down for?"

Polly, hesitantly. "Well, he knew about me and Robert and I didn't want Robert to find out I was married, and then I was kind of sorry for Phil. He was broke and had come out of the pen with bad lungs."

Abrams. "And why did you keep it from Dancer?"

Polly. "It was nobody else's business, and a girl in this racket gets along better without people knowing about things like that."

Abrams. "You didn't know Dancer found out about it, did you?"

Polly. "Not until—" And breaks off with a frightened look at Dancer.

Abrams. "Go ahead—not until what?"

Dancer. "I never found out about it up to now." Then, to Polly. "I wish I had, Baby."

Abrams says to Dancer, "Stick your mouth out of this until you get your invitation. You'll get it." Then to Polly. "And now you think he killed Phil because he found out?"

Polly stammers, "No—I don't—I—"

Abrams breaks in very sharply. "Isn't it the truth, sister, that you and this husband of yours were working together on Robert Landis and something went wrong and you had to kill him?"

Polly shakes her head and says, "No."

Abrams, paying no attention to her answer. "And then isn't it just as true that Dancer found out about it and killed Phil?"

Dancer interrupts again. "Listen, I never found out about it till I come to this room."

Abrams. "Whenever you found out about it, what do you think now—don't you think they were double-crossing you?"

Dancer shrugs and says, "Maybe I do now, but I didn't know anything about it till you told me."

Abrams asks him, "Do you think Phil tried to stick Landis up and had to kill him?"

Dancer replies contemptuously, "I don't know what a punk like that would do."

Abrams' manner has become increasingly irritable through this scene so that when, as he starts to ask Dancer, "Now do you—" and Nick interrupts him by saying, "Let's go into the check business," Abrams turns around and says, sharply for him, "Who's doing this?"

Nick says very mildly, "It's hardly ever been my party. Come on, Nora."

Abrams says very earnestly, "Aw, listen, Mr. Charles, I'm not getting any rest out of this at all and I'm kind of jumpy. What were you going to say?"

Nick. "I thought I said it—about those forgeries?"

Dancer says to Nick, "I've put up with your gum-heeling for a day or two, but I got a business to run. I better be down there running it than barbering here with you. Why don't the two of us just go out in the hall and see who smacks who in the nose and call it square?"

Nick. "No, let's do it the hard way. The ten-grand check Landis is supposed to have given Polly is a forgery."

Dancer. "So what's it to me?"

Nick. "The signature was traced from one of the other checks he gave her."

Dancer. "I'm still asking you—what's that to me?"

Nick. "Maybe Polly can answer that." He asks her, "Did you do the tracing or did he?"

While Polly is hesitating, Dancer says very distinctly, "I told you before, I don't know anything about that check. Whatever was between Landis and Polly was between them."

Nick says to Polly, "You were right—they *are* letting you hold the bag."

Before Polly can answer, Dancer, addressing Nick, but talking for Polly's benefit, asks, "What bag? This check you're talking about—has anybody tried to pass it yet? What kind of charge have you got against her until she does?"

Nick and Abrams look at each other and Abrams says, "Wise guy." Then to Polly. "Come on, answer that question now."

Polly says hesitantly, "Well, I don't know—I—"

She breaks off, looking all the time at Dancer, hoping for a cue.

Dancer says nothing and gives Polly no sign.

Polly. "Honestly, Lieutenant Abrams, I don't think that check is a forgery."

Abrams asks, "Where did you get it?"

Polly. "Well, I—" She breaks off again.

Abrams. "What are you covering this lug up for, sister?" He takes the note David had given him out of his pocket and shows it to her, saying "See, he had already found out Phil was your husband."

Polly reads the note and her eyes widen. She looks at Dancer.

Dancer. "If you're helping to frame me, Polly, okay; I'll have to figure out what I do about that, but if you haven't made a dicker for yourself with the police, I don't see where you'll be getting anywhere just running off at the head for the fun of it."

Abrams starts toward Dancer, saying angrily, "Listen, you—"

The door opens and Caspar comes in. He bows very formally to everybody in the room, then says to Dancer, "I just heard a moment ago." Then, very pompously, to Abrams. "Lieutenant,I cannot permit you to—"

Abrams turns to Nick and groans, "Now, look—we got this five-and-ten-cent-store Darrow with us again."

Caspar says to Nick, "Good evening, Mr. Charles."

Nick bows, buttoning up his coat and patting his pockets to see if he's lost anything.

Caspar goes over to Dancer, puts a hand on his

shoulder, and says, "My dear boy—I'm entirely at your service."

Dancer shakes the hand off his shoulder and snarls, "You ought to be—for the dough you charge me."

Caspar tries to smile as if he thought Dancer were joking. He asks Lum Kee, "What are these policemen doing now?"

Lum Kee, bland as usual, says, "Trouble, trouble—they want to see us—we go—why not? They police, we innocent, you betcha."

Abrams growls, "Aw, cut it out. Hold your conferences on your own time. We've got work to do. Has anybody here ever been in this apartment before?"

Some of those there say "No," some shake their heads.

Abrams looks questioningly at Nick. Nick says, "Perhaps Polly could help us if we told her what it's all about."

Polly. "What?"

Nick. "You know this place is right over yours?"

Polly. "Yes."

Nick, indicating the earpieces. "With that dingus you can hear a pin drop in your place." She stares at the earpieces in surprise. Nick goes on. "And if you'll go to the window, you'll see a ladder running down to your window." She goes to the window, looks at the ladder, then turns back to Nick, still more bewildered. Nick picks up the extra piece of pipe and says, "And nobody's head would be helped much by being patted with this."

Polly. "But I don't understand—"

Nick, looking at Dancer and Lum Kee, says, "Is there anybody here that *does* understand?"

Dancer looks sullenly at him but doesn't say anything.

Lum Kee says cheerfully, "We run restaurant—you detective."

Nick to Polly. "Even if you don't understand, who can you think of that would have this much interest in you?" hefting the pipe in his hand.

Polly. "Nobody."

Nick. "Phil had a key to your apartment. Has Dancer?"

Before she can reply, Dancer takes a key out of his pocket and tosses it on the floor, saying "Yes. So what would I need that trick ladder for?"

Nick asks, "Has Lum Kee?"

Polly. "No, of course not."

Nick. "Who else?"

Polly. "Nobody."

Nick. "Did Robert have one?"

Polly. "No. What do you think I did, put them around under doors?"

A policeman opens the door and Selma comes in. She and Nora immediately run to each other uttering exclamations of affection.

David exclaims, "Selma," and he goes over to them asking, "are you all right, dear?"

She exclaims, "David," and, holding out her hands to him, she starts to ask him a question, "Did you—" and then breaks off, glancing nervously at Lieutenant Abrams. "Oh, it's been terrible," she tells Nora and David.

Nora. "I know, dear, but it'll soon be over. Nick will have everything cleared up in no time. He's wonderful."

Nick. "Nice of you to say so, darling." He goes over to greet Selma.

Selma. "Oh Nick, I'm so grateful to you. Have you really—?"

Nick. "Now don't start asking us questions. The game is for us to ask you. Have you ever seen any of these people before?" indicating in turn Polly, Dancer, and Lum Kee. To each Selma replies "No."

Nick asks, "Have you ever been in this building before?"

Selma. "No."

Nick. "Did you know that Robert and Miss Byrnes were friends?"

Selma. "No."

Nick. "All right. Now this next question you've answered before, but the police weren't altogether satisfied with the way you answered it. I want you to remember that Robert's dead, so whatever you say isn't going to hurt him though it may help us find his murderer and get you out of this mess."

Selma. "What is it, Nick?"

Nick. "That ten-thousand-dollar check of yours that was deposited in Robert's account. Did you or didn't you write it?"

Selma hesitates, looks from Nick to Abrams, then down to the floor, and, in a very low voice, says, "I didn't."

Abrams, who has been a very interested listener up to this point, now takes his hat off and throws it angrily on the floor. But when he crosses to confront Selma,

107

his voice and manner are more hurt than angry. He asks, "Why couldn't you have told us that before? Whatever got into you to—" He breaks off as her lips begin to tremble, and grabs a chair, saying "Now, now, sit down, Mrs. Landis, be comfortable. One of you boys get Mrs. Landis a glass of water." Then again to her. "Now, now, maybe there's not a great deal of harm done anyhow." Then aside to Nick, as she sits down. "If this dame gets hysterical again, I'll go nuts."

Selma. "Thank you. I'm quite all right."

Abrams mumbles in Nick's ear, "You ask her the rest. She always blows up on me."

Nick says to Selma, "Since you've gone this far, I think you'd better tell the police why you didn't tell them the truth before."

Selma. "I started to, but Aunt Katherine wouldn't let me."

Abrams growls, "That old battle-axe."

Nick asks, "Why wouldn't she?"

Selma. "She said there was enough scandal with Robert being killed that way, without this."

Nick. "Thanks. That's fine." Pats her on the shoulder, turns away.

Abrams. "Maybe that's fine for you, but it could stand a little more explaining for my part."

Nick. "The explaining room is out there," indicating the kitchen. "Shall we try it now?" He and Abrams go into the kitchen. Nick continues, "The gadget is that Aunt Katherine thought Robert forged the check and she was willing to let the ten thousand dollars go to keep people from knowing there had been

a forger in the family as well as a murdered man—"
Then, as an afterthought, he adds, "Especially since
it was Selma's ten thousand."

Abrams asks, "Had he ever done anything like that
before?"

Nick, earnestly. "That boy had done everything."

Francis comes to the door and says, "Telephone for
you," to Abrams.

Abrams goes out.

Nick spies a battered cocktail shaker on the shelf
and begins to look through the closets for something
to put in it. The closets are absolutely bare. He disgustedly throws the cocktail shaker in the garbage can
as Abrams comes back.

Abrams. "The laboratory says those red hairs were
probably from a wig and that the broken specs were
only window glass. Were you kind of expecting something like that?"

Nick. "Kinda."

Abrams. "And the gun's not the one those people
were killed with. Expect that?"

Nick. "Kinda."

Abrams. "But what's really good is, the boys picked
up some pretty nice fingerprints of Dancer's in the
joint. Let's go in and see how he likes that."

Nick. "All right, but mind if I get in a question
first?"

Abrams. "Go ahead, help yourself."

They return to the room where the others are.

Nick asks Lum Kee, "Did you ever mail to Mrs.

Landis a compact that you thought she left in the restaurant about a week ago?"

Lum Kee. "Maybe yes, maybe no. All the time people leave things."

Nick to Dancer. "I knew he didn't. You sent it to her pretending you thought it was hers and when she sent it back with a note saying it wasn't, you traced her signature on the bottom of a ten-thousand-dollar check payable to Robert, and sent it over for deposit in his account because you knew the bank wouldn't question that and when they eventually found out it was a forgery, he'd be blamed for it because he'd done things like that before. Then you were all set to forge a check on his account for the same ten thousand while Polly kept him busy so that the bank couldn't reach him to ask him about it if they got suspicious. And so then if he's killed, who's going to be able to prove that he didn't forge his wife's name to the check to get money to give to this girl he was in love with?"

Dancer asks scornfully, "And then I suppose I knock him off and stir up all this fuss before I get the dough? What kind of a stumblebum does that make me out to be?"

Nick. "I'll let you know in a little while. Take the witness, Lieutenant Abrams."

Abrams. "I'll tell you what kind of a stumblebum you are. You're the kind that left fingerprints all over Phil Byrnes' joint when you killed him."

Caspar comes forward between Dancer and Abrams, saying "Lieutenant Abrams, I cannot allow—"

Dancer takes him by the back of the neck and pushes

him out of the way, snarling "Shut up! Everything *you* say is used against *me*." Then to Abrams, "Yeah, I was at Phil's place last night and when I left he was on the floor with a split lip and a goog and a couple of dents in him here and there, but he was just as alive as you are, if that means anything."

Abrams. "You mean you went up there when you had the switch pulled in your place?"

Dancer. "Yeah."

Abrams. "What for?"

Dancer looks thoughtful for a moment, then says, "Okay, I don't know what I'm letting myself in for, but I'm not going to let you hang any murder rap on me. This Robert was a sucker and Polly and I were taking him. Maybe it was some kind of check razzle-dazzle like he (jerking a thumb at Nick) said maybe it wasn't. Even if it had been, what would be the sense of killing him? Nobody'd have believed him if he'd said he hadn't forged his wife's name. Maybe we even talked him into doing it; anyways, he's cooled before we get anything. This guy," jerking his thumb again at Nick, "says Phil followed Robert and Polly down the street. Knowing Phil, I figured he tried to stick Robert up that night and had had to kill him. I don't like having a punk gum things up for me that way, so why shouldn't I go over and push him around a little to learn him manners. But I didn't kill him."

Abrams asks, "Did you ever wear a wig?"

Dancer seems completely surprised. Then he says, "No, but you ought to see my collection of hoopskirts."

Abrams asks Lum Kee, "Did you?"

Lum Kee says, "No," pulling a lock of his hair. "Good hair—see?"

Abrams groans and says to Nick, "I *hate* comedians." Then he asks Polly, "Did you?"

Polly. "No."

Abrams. "Have you thought of anything that might have something to do with this layout?" indicating the window from which ladder is hanging, and earphones.

Polly. "No. But maybe this was all just a gag. Nobody came down and hit me on the head with that pipe and Robert wasn't killed in my place."

Nick asks her, "You know why that was, don't you?"

Polly. "No."

Francis says to detective standing beside him, "What a swell gal she'd be to take out—all she can say is 'No.'"

Nick. "I'll tell you. This mysterious Anderson, probably in a red wig, phony glasses, and gloves to keep from leaving fingerprints, was sitting up here at his listening post waiting for a good chance to come down and polish off Robert, and hearing most of the things that were said down there between you and Phil and you and Dancer and you and Robert, until he knew more about all of you than any of *you* did. But for one reason or another, he put off the killing until he learned that you and Robert were going away the next day. It was that night or never with him, but he got a bad break. Pedro came up and wanted to put a new rug down. That would have exposed the listening post and spoiled everything; so when he tries to talk Pedro out of it—"

Asta, who has been playing with David over by the open window, now lifts his leg against the chair.

Nora yells, "Asta!" Then complains, "Now I'll have to take you out just when I was so interested. Couldn't you wait until I get back, Nicky?"

David. "I'll take him out for you."

Nick to Abrams. "Murderers get funnier every year, don't they?"

Abrams. "Huh?"

Nick. "Just when you get ready to arrest them, they want to take dogs out walking!"

Everybody looks at Nick in surprise.

Nick. "David is Anderson. He didn't recognize Pedro any more than Robert or I did, but in spite of the disguise Pedro finally recognized him, just as Polly told us he'd recognized Robert. I suppose David gave him some hocus-pocus story, but Pedro, knowing Robert was spending a lot of time in the apartment just below this, probably knowing that Robert married Selma and knowing that David had been engaged to her when Pedro was working for Nora, and knowing Nora married a detective, thought he'd better change the lock and keep David out until he could come over and ask Nora's and my advice. He was foolish enough to tell David what he was going to do and David followed him over and shot him in the vestibule."

David turns to Nora, who is standing beside him by the window, and asks, "Nora, is he fooling?"

Nora says nothing. She is too busy listening to Nick, as are the others.

Nick. "Sure. And *you* were fooling when you said you hadn't seen him since he worked for Nora and pretended you remembered him as a man with a long gray mustache. He's got one now all right, but if you'll look at that picture downstairs, you'll see that it was neither very long nor very gray then. And what was Phil doing on your fire escape except to try to shake you down because we know he'd followed you and Polly that night? We know the boy liked to shake people down; but you weren't alone that night, so he beat it and made a date with you for the next night and got himself killed."

David protests, "But—"

Nick, paying no attention to him, continues "—and what do you suppose Pedro was trying to say when he died? That he'd been killed by *Miss Selma's young man*, which would be a servant's language for your status back when he worked for Nora."

Selma says, "But Nick, why should David have killed him? He'd given him the bonds and Robert was going away."

Nick. "He didn't want Robert to go away—he wanted to kill him. That's why he had to do it that night; otherwise he'd have had to hunt all over the world for him. Promising to pay him, with Polly knowing it, would make it look as though he had no reason for killing him. He intended killing him that night he met him, but Polly was along, so he couldn't. But he followed him and shot him when he came out of the house."

Selma. "I can't believe—"

David grabs Nora and forces her backward out of the window so that only her legs are inside and she is

114

held there only by his arms. His face has become insane, his voice, high-pitched and hysterical. He screams,
"I'm not going to the gallows! Either you give me your
word that I go out of here with a five-minute start, or
Nora goes out of the window with me."

The policemen's guns are in their hands, but everyone is afraid to move except Lum Kee, who, standing
by the corridor door, softly slips out, and Selma, who
starts toward David, crying "David!"

David snarls, "Keep away, you idiot!"

Nick, talking to gain time, trying not to show how
frightened he is, says to Selma, "See, he's not in love
with you. He was, but when you turned him down for
Robert, he probably came to hate you almost as much
as he did Robert. But playing the faithful lover let him
hang around until he could get a crack at Robert.
That's why when he saw you hop around the corner
with a gun in your hand right after he'd shot Robert
from the car, he circled the block and came back in
time to frame you while he pretended he was covering
you up. He had probably meant to frame Phil or
Dancer—which he did after he'd had to kill Phil while
you were in jail."

David, from the window, says, "You're stalling for
time, Nick, and it's no good. Five minutes' start or
another of your lovely family goes down on the rocks
with me."

Nick. "Don't be a sap, David. The chances are
they'd never hang you. You ought to be able to get off
with a few years in an asylum. What jury's going to
believe a sane man did all this?"

stocking feet. He is standing in a puddle. He smiles blandly and says, "I go down and get my shoes," while Nora exclaims reproachfully, "Asta!"

After the Thin Man *was released fifteen months after the story published here was completed. During the process of preparing a final script, there was one major alteration in the plot.*

The produced movie omits the murder of Pedro Dominges at the beginning. Instead, Nick finds Pedro's body in the basement of the apartment house where Polly lives when he goes there to inspect her apartment after Robert has been murdered. While there, Nick finds the compact sent to Selma and her signed note returning it. Her signature on the note was the model for the forged check on her account. As Nick is leaving, Dancer comes in and a gun battle ensues, without injury to either party and without either man seeing the other's face. Dancer flees through the basement, Nick chasing him. There Nick finds a trunk with Pedro's body inside. In the movie, Pedro is demoted from his implausible position as owner of the apartment house to janitor.

The ending in the movie version is also altered slightly. Lum Kee still saves Nora's life, but again a measure of plausibility is added. Instead of holding Nora out the window, David pulls a gun and holds it to her head. Lum Kee pitches his hat into David's face, covering his eyes, and the gun is forced from David's hand. The joke about Lum Kee liking his brother's girl rather than his brother remains, and David is taken in custody by Lieutenant Abrams.

Most of the dialogue in the movie was supplied by the screenwriters, Albert Hackett and Frances Goodrich. Hammett's contribution was plot and mood.

A Friend to the Limit

JEFFRY SCOTT

*Jeffry Scott is better known to British readers as
journalist Shaun Usher, entertainment writer and
television critic for* The London Daily Sketch *until
1972, and more recently for the* London Daily
Mail. *With his father, journalist and author Gray
Usher, he has edited two collections of stories
about the supernatural—*The Graveyard Companion *(1975), and* Festival of Fiends *(1976). As Jeffry Scott, he has written a mystery novel,* Trust
Them and Die *(1969) Jeffry Scott has twice won
the Crime Writers Association prize for the best
short story of the year, in 1972 and 1973.*

TERRY MCNAIR's a good enough kid in his
way. Dumb rather than stupid, the dumb-
ness of inexperience—seventeen's the age for that.

Rick McNair and his son had moved into the next
apartment a few months back. Terry would run errands,
wash my car, feed the cats and like that, all without a
handful of "gimme." He just liked feeling useful, helping out. Right now he was about to help his old man
into an early grave.

I don't snoop worth a damn, but this time it was hard to resist. Their apartment door was open, and locking mine, I heard sounds that wouldn't mean diddly to some folk and said plenty to me. The small noises certain types of machined metal make when you treat them a certain way.

Ready to duck, I put my head round the door. Sure enough, Rick McNair had a handgun there, a big old Colt model 1911, your basic .45 automatic. I'd heard him smacking the magazine home and now he worked the slide and set the safety and put the piece down the back of his jeans; kind of shrugged and wriggled, making sure it set right, and got into a parka. It was loose enough for the gun to be hidden.

"Yo, Rick," says I, because he'd looked up and caught me peeking. "Gonna rob a liquor store or what?"

"Norm, just mind your own business and leave me mind mine," McNair told me. He was at the door by then. The faint smell of work sweat—he was a carpenter—had that overlay of anger, a coppery reek. He was looking past me, not at anything solid, but what he meant to do next.

"Sure thing," I agreed, stepping aside to show sincerity. "Only you're from out of state. . . . Maybe you aren't aware that in *this* state they're kind of into gun control and suchlike. Kinky for permits. Get caught on the street with that piece, you'll take a long vacation, all your fellow guests be wearing the selfsame clothes, eating the same meals, if you get my drift."

Rick McNair stared at me until I came into focus. A lot of stuff was going on behind his poker face. I gave him credit for it not being that the last thing he needed was some nosy black dude giving him a short course on firearms regs in the city.

"I don't aim to get caught," he said. "Appreciate your concern though, Norm. But this is fam'ly business."

He's a widower with just the one kid, meaning the business concerned young Terry McNair. It was then I noticed Terry in a corner of the living room. He looked pale and sort of sickly, and he's one healthy kid.

McNair nodded like I'd said something. "Yeah, the jackass got himself a heap of trouble, over the Limit."

"Makes sense," I said. The Limit's a couple—two, three blocks on Republican and the itty cross streets between aforesaid blocks. Every city has a Times Square or Combat Zone. Here we call it the Limit. *Good* place to stay away from, 'less you work out of there. Me, I visit some. But up on my tippy-toes, one set of eyes doing duty for maybe four sets.

"Kid got a heap of trouble, and now you going there?" Ricky McNair nodded, zipped up the parka, understood that hampered the pistol, unzipped it again. White folks listen, oftentimes they don't bother hearing. I'd told the man something, he cared to think about it. So I had to go the *i*-dotting, *t*-crossing route. "What you plan on doing, down there at the Limit?"

"Kick ass," said McNair. "Get Terry's money back. Dumb kid!" Biting down on the anger, he managed a little grin. "It's not the principle of the thing, Norm. It's the money, right?"

"I can save that much again, easy," Terry put in. His left cheek was red and the ear real fiery red. I figured Pop had smacked him upside the head, a good one. "It's only a hundred dollars."

"The hell it's only a hundred dollars; where d'you come off with the 'only,' Mr. Rockefeller?" McNair went, top of his voice. And to me: "Kid's spent best part of a year saving that; he wants a motorcycle. Then he gets a better idea, whorin' around this Limit place. Where's it at, anyway?"

"You try kicking ass around the Limit, all they'll find is your foot, they put that in some kind of museum," I told McNair. "I mean it, Rick. Cops go in double-banked, riot guns for walking canes. You want the Limit that bad, ask some other sucker."

Ten minutes later, out front, Rick McNair stopped fooling with what he calls wheels—little rust bucket near as old as his son—and came over. Me, I'm laid back on my reclining seat in reclined mode, nice tunes on the stereo, ready to motorvate, no particular place to go.

"Listen," McNair said, "lend me your car, Norm. Please. Mine won't start, damn it." Naturally, on account of me fixing it that way.

"This fine car don't go to no Limit," I announced, giving him a little ethnic rasp in the voice. "But I'll give you and Terry a ride."

He nodded tautlike. "Get in the back," he ordered Terry, and slid in beside me. It took a while to get to the Limit, plenty of home-going traffic that time of day. "When did he go, anyway?" I asked Rick McNair.

"This afternoon, fourish," Terry supplied from the back. That struck me as a little early for the locality, like five, six hours early. The Limit's hardly begun hopping by nine at night.

"I was just curious," Terry mumbled. "And I heard about this ace girl there, she . . . well, you know . . . does it. I was curious."

"A hooker," his father snapped.

Not looking at either of them, I said, "Rick, *you* never had anything to do with a lady of the night, huh? Not in Nam or wherever? Real straight arrow, my man."

"Not at Terry's age," McNair said shortly. "Not hardly ever. Never, once I'd met his mother, God rest her soul."

"I was curious," Terry whined. "All the guys were talking about the Limit, what goes on there."

"They go all the time, huh?" I suggested.

Terry started to say yes, but he's an honest kid and after a bit he said, "Well, some of them. One guy, anyway. His father's a landlord there, so Mike gets left alone."

"Fine friends you make," McNair said.

"He's not a friend, we were just hanging out, talking," Terry explained miserably.

"This looks a decent area," his father said, when I pulled in. "I thought the Limit—"

"This aint it," I said. "From here we walk. Limit's down there a ways, and one block over. Rick, either you let me lock that forty-five piece in the trunk or . . . put it this way, you pull it for any reason at all, I'll bust your hand before you get to squeeze a shot off. You can bank on that in Denver, my friend."

He just grunted and got out of the car. He thought I was bragging, but that was all right because I knew I wasn't—and that left the pair of us happy.

Rule of thumb: Carry a piece and sooner or later you have to use it or get dead. Dumbest dumb in my book. Around the Limit, it's likely to be sooner than later, at that. Plenty of mean characters there, choice of race and all three sexes, count 'em.

We went over to Republican and pretty soon the discount and novelty stores were empty stores, hole-in-wall head shops, peep shows, places showing triple-X movies and promising live action on stage between whiles. Dross City, no question.

Cross streets, being narrower and darker, were worse. But the quarter was empty, still asleep. Fairly safe, especially with three of us teamed.

"It was in there," Terry said, after leading us down the wrong street and trying again. He pointed at a brownstone, some of the upper windows shuttered with marine ply sheets, ripe for the demo men. At street level, a dusty-windowed store showed a few items of the type of leisurewear that comes with spikes and studs. It hadn't seen a customer since when and the lights were out.

"Not so fast." I towed the pair of them into an alley beside the brownstone. "How'd you come to lose the money, get robbed, Terry? She do it up in her crib? You get mugged out here on the sidewalk? What?"

"I never saw the girl," he told me. "Mike showed me

where she operates, gave me a ride to school this morning, we cut through here on the way. I came back, solo, this afternoon. Street door doesn't lock, you can shove it open. Her place is on the third floor.

"It's dark, no windows on the stairs, the lights don't work. I got to the landing, saw her apartment door. I was . . . um . . . getting up courage, I guess. Somebody jumped me from behind, slammed me against the wall so hard I saw stars, my nose bled. Uh, they twisted my arm, too, slammed me again, ran away. I heard them on the stairs. Then I found my money was gone."

Rick McNair shook his head in disgust.

"Where was the wallet?" I asked.

"Back pocket of my jeans. I know, I know, it's a stupid place to carry a wallet, Norm."

"You learned that the hard way, it'll stick." It cheered him up some. "The guy who jumped you, what he look like?"

Terry's blush made his whole face match the red ear. "All I know . . . it was a man. He was behind me all the time, then I was on the floor when he took off. You could tell it was a man, from the feel of his hands when he grabbed me, twisted my arm and all."

"Okay, mystery man clobbers you. Maybe he was waiting, maybe he followed you in. What next? Hooker come out, ask what goes on? He's bouncing you off walls hard enough to draw blood, must've been a ruckus."

"I just wanted to get the hell out of there." Terry turned to his father. "Look, Mike kind of dared me and . . . I was curious and I didn't want to seem a nerd, you know? I took money to show her, string her along, but I meant to duck out before . . . well, anything. Then I could tell the guys I'd been there, prove it by saying what she and her place looked like."

"We're wasting time," Rick McNair grumbled. "The girl's pimp waits for morons like this one, too green and puny to matter, and roughs 'em up, lifts their dough. Let's get to it, Norm. You stay here."

"No way, José. We'll all go up there, visit a spell." I was thinking that Rick McNair might be hell on wheels as a carpenter but he couldn't figure worth diddly. No hooker's main man carries on that way. He do, word travels among the johns pretty soon his girl runs out of clients. For sure. Maybe he does knock over a fat-cat john every so often. But wise birds don't foul their own nests and hookers' men are real owls when it comes to their trade. They hit the john down the block a piece, never the doorstep.

Like Terry said, the street door looked solid but pushed open. By the second set of stairs, I was climbing them real slow, feeling less than good—and I'm in shape.

When I glanced back, Terry said, "Yeah, there's a terrible smell. Plain dirt, I guess. That would have put me off, even if I hadn't decided to duck out soon as I saw her, from the start."

I hardly heard him. Rick McNair was staring up at me over the kid's shoulder. He and I knew that smell, you never forget it. Somebody nearby was dead, and had been that way for too long.

McNair pushed past his son and then me. We

reached the famous landing. He went to press the buzzer beside the apartment door but I stepped in fast. "Don't touch a thing, Rick. Terry, you go back to the stairs, keep watch."

I just wanted him well out of the way. Any fool could tell that the brownstone was deserted, waiting for the wrecker's ball. That store at street level had been shut for weeks and the ex-owner hadn't bothered to haul the window-display merchandise away. Street people had been using the hallway for a rest room; the odor up here wasn't so much worse than lower down, just different. . . .

The lock was strictly five-and-dime; I slipped it with a credit card.

We didn't have to go in.

The woman was just inside. She hadn't been much in life and was even less now. I couldn't tell whether she had been strangled or what, the corpse was far gone. Maybe it had been there for a week. The rats hadn't helped anything but themselves, the way rats will.

"Jesus," Rick McNair groaned, and it wasn't taking holy names in vain. "Let's get out of here."

The apartment, as I'd expected, was empty. The floor was fluffy tan underlay, the final tenant had ripped up the carpet. Unfaded places on the walls showed where furniture must have stood. I stood firm as McNair yanked my arm.

"Stuff to do," I told him.

"Say what?" He didn't realize it, but he was shouting.

"Terry's wallet must be around here." He blinked

126

at me and I got mad. "Come on, Rick! Terry couldn't kill a fly and somebody suckered him here next a body." Then I heard that yowl-whoop-yowl cutting off suddenly, maybe a block away.

Great.

Now there was all of sixty seconds to do a day's work. The stairway had no windows but the apartment couldn't get by without them. I yelled for Terry to get in there with us—he went green and started to take off at the sight of the dead lady but McNair grabbed him.

I wrestled the nearest window open. "Fire escape," I told McNair. "Don't go down! Go up and over the roof, far as you can get. Use cover, go quiet, think Nam. Terry, this kid Mike—what car he drive? Quick, boy!"

He was nauseous, fighting it, eyes rolling. I shook him. "What car?"

"Uh . . . uh . . . Toyota. Silver, black roof."

"Go!" I whacked McNair's rump, nearly threw Terry out after him onto the rusty iron escape route of the fire stairs.

The apartment being stripped cut searching time. Terry's wallet was half under the body, shoved there. I ripped it out, frantically checking the contents. Money, tickets for a rock concert, some clippings from *Sports Illustrated*.

Either he'd been cool enough to leave his ID at home, which I doubted, or Terry simply kept it separate from his dough. Adding my cash to the wallet, I slipped it into my jacket pocket, using the now-empty money clip, a hammered silver-dollar sign, to fix tie to shirt.

I just finished when two cops burst in. You can climb stairs fast or quiet; they'd tried both at once and could be heard on the final flight. So I was reaching way up, grabbing air, a fraction *before* they made the scene.

They said I was in a lot of trouble and a bad person to boot. Not hardly, I said, but polite.

What it was, I told them, I'd been hanging out on the corner and noticed this white teenager, maybe high school, in a silver Toyota with a black roof. He'd been in and out of the brownstone here, half a dozen times in a matter of hours. Made a fellow think. . . .

Just now, I said, I'd gone into the hallway of the building to take a leak, and the same kid came barreling down the stairs, never seeing me in the shadows. So I'd decided to snoop around, see what drew him upstairs, day after day.

Sure, I'd opened the window. Had they noticed the smell in there? No, I didn't know the dead lady from Adam, and neither would anyone, bar her Maker, thanks to those rats. But I did know that yellow simulated leather coat. Belonged on a street lady I'd seen from time to time, on the next block to here. . . .

Finally the brightest cop ran out to their car, got on the switch about his comrades looking out for a black-and-silver Toyota driven by a kid. Later this cop told me he'd been covering all the bases and figured the vehicle and driver to be figments of my imagination.

Only while he was still leaning into the police car,

he saw a black-and-silver Toyota cruise past; stayed cool, and observed it was driving round and round the block.

Which was how Terry's friend Mike, who knew the Limit so well, came to be detained as well as me.

Mike's story ran that he happened to be driving past, that was all. He denied pointing out the building to Terry McNair or telling him a hooker was there.

But as I'd gambled, Rick McNair had just enough smarts to take off on a sudden visit to Vermont with Terry. Well, I hadn't figured Vermont, just far and fast until the mud settled. Okay, it was schooltime. Then again, it's the American way, Pop and Junior going off to fish and hunt. Rick McNair was an impulsive father, what can I tell you?

Until they caught up with father and son, the cops had to be satisfied with me and Mike the Toyota driver. Even with his dad's lawyer present, Mike made an uneasy witness. Then they matched his voiceprints to the anonymous call on 911, claiming a murder at the brownstone, and the prints matched.

This made Mike an uneasier witness. His lawyer had a long talk with him, in private. Then the plea bargaining began, Mike 'fessed up—he'd hit on the street lady, greased her in a panic when she refused to get out of the car again, wanting extra cash—and I was released. My fine car had been towed, like to wrecked the transmission. The Good Samaritan never had that breed of static, but then again, I guess in those Bible times he'd have ridden a mule.

About two days later Rick McNair phoned me, kind

of high-strung and guarded in his talk. "Relax, come on home," I said. "No problem anymore."

In the middle of the night, Rick McNair and Terry were hammering at my door. Thank you, thank you, how in the world did you figure it, so forth. How in the world could anyone *not* figure it, I nearly came back at them.

Mike had been on the prod for Terry to go to the apartment where he'd dumped the body. From the speed the cops turned up, somebody had been watching the place, ready to tip them when we went in. It was such a rinky-dink, schoolyard plotting affair. . . .

As such, there was a good chance, far better than drawing to a straight, that the someone who'd called the cops would hang around the neighborhood to see how his caper worked out. Amateurs always want to make sure, that's how they stay amateurs, right?

Which was why I needed to know what sort of car Mike drove. If I'd been wrong about Mike, then it was my grief. Any fool could tell the street lady had been dead more than forty-eight hours, and I'd only been back in the city for a day—before that, I'd been in Vegas for nine days. Very firmly in, thank you: in jail, to be exact. The worst the cops could have done was give me a hard time.

So it was all pretty simple, considering. When I said simple, Rick McNair gave me a look as much as to say I was fooling. He was a good guy and Terry was a good kid, but they weren't swift.

Rick McNair hugged me hard, close to tears. "Anything you ever want and it's in my power, you got it, Norm."

"One thing, then, right now. That .45 piece, Rick—toss it in the river. As a favor to me, huh?" He wanted to know why, now the trouble had passed, but I stalled on that and Rick went off to fulfill his promise.

I couldn't tell him that I might not be able to watch out for him another time. Or that some white folks just can't handle pressure.

Frisbee in the Middle

R. D. BROWN

R. D. Brown is a professor of English at Western Washington University. His mystery novel Prime Suspect, *a paperback original published by Belmont-Tower in 1981, has been republished by Dorchester Publishing Company.*

Besides frequent contributions to Ellery Queen's Mystery Magazine, *Professor Brown has a long list of academic publications, including* The Heritage of Romanticism *(1983), and* Guide to Better Themes *(with Robert A. Peters, 1970).*

GLENDORA DROPPED IT on my blotter where it spun like a top while she talked.

"He says his name is Schmettler."

Glendora is almost the perfect secretary. She's prettier than a red pickup, but she has a mind like a computer. That means she presents facts, follows instructions to the letter, and only offers conclusions when asked. Sometimes, that makes her a little irritating. Like now, when some Godzilla tears the knob off our office door to show he's eager to do business, she makes him give her his name before delivering the message. Why? Because I once said I liked to know who wanted to talk to me.

"The man with him didn't say anything, but he should probably be indicted for the way he looked at me."

As you would imagine, Glendora is doing very well in law school. Between classes, she helps out as a secretary while I turn over enough skip tracing to pay the rent and cover her tuition. Evenings, we discuss the US Tax Code and other fun things. When she passes the bar exam, we'll set up as Biggart and Frisbee, Corporation Taxation Specialists. She'll handle the trial work, while I do research in the back room because I want, but seldom get, a tranquil life.

It had been a slow week, so I was willing to forgive Mr. Schmettler's enthusiasm. The knob was still spinning, just now starting to show the occasional wobble.

"Think of this as opportunity knocking," I told her.

When Schmettler came through the doorway like a transcontinental truck on a one-lane bridge, I changed my mind, not about him, but the bad news that came as part of the package, a little fellow about five feet high with a bad reputation about twice as tall.

The last I heard, Arnie Buttons had been under indictment on seventeen counts of larceny, counterfeiting, procuring, trafficking in controlled substances, felony, murder, and suspicion of worshiping graven images. A slow week had become a bad one.

"We don't want any," I said, standing up to move in front of Glendora while Arnie looked around the office and decided not to buy it.

"Get the broad out of this dump," he said.

Personally, I find our decor is very pleasant; rental furniture, true, but not too much of it. I didn't quarrel with his taste, though I did take charge of the situation.

"I don't think these people want coffee, Glendora, but I do. Double cream with a prune Danish."

Glendora is brighter than I am, but before she met me, she had to spend a lot of time pretending to be dumb. She did it now, popping some nonexistent chewing gum and flouncing out of the room after a wide-eyed look at our guests.

When the door closed behind her, Arnie brought me up to speed. "You're a hunter. The best. I want you to hunt somebody."

"I'm a finder," I said. "A hunter goes for blood, but I like solving puzzles. If you want to get in touch with somebody on a civil cause, I'm your man. I serve processes, catch bail jumpers, repossess cars, and find wandering spice, but nothing more."

Arnie picked up the doorknob and Schmettler looked interested. "I know about you, Frisbee. You don't play in the traffic these days. Take a walk, Bruno."

Schmettler lost interest in me. Since his boss hadn't told him to remove it, he left the knob on the inner door as he left. Arnie sat down in the client chair.

"I got a target you might like. Looey Flowers."

I had reasons not to like Looey Flowers, almost as many as I had to dislike Arnie Buttons. They were two of a kind, and until I came along, they'd been rivals in the same organization. But Looey had taken out a competitor in front of a witness, an innocent citizen who had the bad luck to be present when Looey was acting out with a sawed-off shotgun. Being of normal intelligence, the witness left the area fast.

The state attorney gave me the job of finding him. I did, five hundred miles off and two weeks later. After I brought him back, he was put in protective custody. The story was he managed to climb out a tiny bathroom window to throw himself out of a hotel suite also occupied by three policemen. I left the business because he rightly prophesied when I took him in that I was signing his death warrant.

After that, with a kind of irony I still don't appreciate, things worked out. Once he was in jail, Looey decided to recite his memoirs. On the basis of the stories he told under immunity, he should have been chained to a rock for all eternity for birds to peck at, but he did something that made it worthwhile. He nailed Arnie Buttons—but good. I wondered why Arnie wasn't in jail. He watched my memory banks work through all this dreck.

"They had to reduce my bail because Looey is the only witness left against me. The rest of them came down with amnesia or absence. That's why I'm hiring you."

Just then the phone rang. Glendora was calling from the café across the street.

"You don't drink coffee, and you never touch refined sugar. I conclude you want me to do something. What?"

"Take the afternoon off," I said, making the automatic protective move that this liberated woman frequently finds vexing. "Mr. Buttons is just leaving."

"Oh!" she said in a startled voice.

"Don't hang up the phone, Bruno," Buttons called across the room. "Mr. Frisbee and I will get back to you in a few minutes."

I've been dealing with middle-class types lately, so I'm out of practice. Arnie had enjoyed demonstrating that. Despite my views on the subject, it was in the cards that I was going to have to find Looey Flowers so Buttons could kill him.

Arnie opened the haggling by saying "She's cute, your secretary."

He paused to let my mind fill with an X-rated movie that would be banned in Port Said.

"You find Flowers, you get ten big ones and the broad back in one piece. You don't, and—ahh—let's not talk about it."

I had some violent thoughts myself, which involved tightening Arnie's necktie till his eyeballs popped out to join the doorknob on my desk. But that wouldn't help Glendora.

"Okay, Arnie. Glendora goes someplace safe where neither of us can reach her or it's no deal."

He didn't like the sound of that, and he fingered his necktie, nervous about the way I was glaring at him.

I explained. Glendora was to go immediately to the YWCA. After she talked to me on the phone from there, I'd look for Flowers. I pointed out that as long as she was in his hands, I had no reason to trust him. Because Arnie knew me pretty well and he very badly needed Flowers dead, he told Schmettler to take her to the YWCA.

While we waited for Glendora's return call, Arnie gave me the story till now. The federal strike force marshals had kept Flowers secure during his testimony by bringing him from the local air base to the roof of the courthouse via helicopter. By the time Arnie's people had discovered Flowers was being kept at the base infirmary, the hearings were over and Flowers had vanished.

Then he told me why it was impossible for Looey to vanish as he did. Arnie's security around the base was perfect: tape monitors on all the exit gates, a radio and telephone watch; even people watching the flight lines. Still, Flowers was gone, and Arnie couldn't understand it.

"How do you know he's gone?"

"His protection left—all those marshals. Somehow, they did it. And don't say he just slipped by us. Looey weighs in over three hundred pounds and getting bigger. They couldn't hide him in a flyboy uniform or get him in the trunk of a car, but they faked me out somehow." He paused to let me see the glint of switchblades in his eyes. "This is important to me, Frisbee!"

As long as Glendora was at risk, it was important to me, too, which I didn't need to tell him. I was wondering how I could keep from being instrumental in Looey's violent demise. Then Glendora phoned from the YWCA, wondering why she was in the penalty box while I had all the fun.

"Some fun," I said. "Either I find Looey Flowers

or someone near and dear has bad trouble. Listen carefully and maybe you can help. Arnie says Looey left the air base. Anyway, a solid ring of Arnie's men say they didn't see him. All the gates were covered, the flight lines, and Looey's too big to go into a car trunk."

"Are you sure he's gone?"

"Arnie tells me the federal marshals left."

"You mean Mr. Flowers evaded all Mr. Button's people?"

"No, I think he avoided them. It's a case of how you hide a three-hundred-pound gorilla who belongs in jail. I expect to find Looey by this afternoon or tomorrow at the latest. Take care. Arnie promised me ten big ones, but don't count the money till I phone again."

Glendora went "humph!" and hung up. Arnie was thoughtful. "Why you telling her all this?"

"She's my auxiliary brain. If I can't figure it out, she can." For the moment, I felt pretty confident.

When Schmettler lumbered in, I could see that Arnie had reason to be confident too.

"I forgot to tell you," he said. "Bruno goes with you. Everywhere. And my people will be all around the YWCA. Maybe I couldn't catch Looey, but I can sure catch a broad."

I wondered what other surprises were upcoming, but I didn't bother to ask because Arnie was no more into full disclosure than I was.

"Let's go, Bruno," I said. We did, in one of those black limousines Arnie was so fond of. Bruno drove me out Claiborne Avenue to an Army and Navy Store that's been there as long as I can remember. A retired first shirt from maybe the War of 1812 runs it.

Fortunately, I was wearing black shoes. While Bruno inspected camping equipment, I bought a shirt and pants in blue cotton wash material and a web belt. I didn't need a cap. The owner was pretty bored till I started sorting through the samples of military decorations.

"You got authorization for those things, Mac?"

Bruno joined us. The owner shut up when Bruno started making speech. "Why you buying all this war surplus, Frisbee?"

"Looey vanished from the air base. That's where I start looking. I want to fit in." I turned back to the ancient clerk.

"I want one of those, one of those, and that neat red one with the white stripes." I'd pointed out ribbons for the Distinguished Flying Cross, the Air Medal, and the Good Conduct badge. The clerk gave me a sour look and said he'd run them up in the back room.

I put on the shirt and pants and inspected electronic gear that was sold by the pound while Schmettler went back to the camping equipment. The clerk returned ten minutes later, in a dead heat with a couple of air police, a sergeant and a corporal.

"This the guy trying to impersonate a hero?" the sergeant said, as much to me as anybody.

When Schmettler came up to see what was going on, the APs undid the flaps of their holsters.

"Who's this guy?" the sergeant wanted to know.

"You may well ask," I told him.

But the sergeant didn't like my answers when he asked for leave papers and dog tags. Then he noted I wore no cap and consequently was out of uniform.

Without any further ado, they shoved me ungently into the air police jeep and away we went. Schmettler pursued us in the black limo and only broke off at the main gate. In the provost marshal's office, I was cooperative but not too talky. They had about decided to nail me for impersonation until the provost asked if I had a serial number.

When I gave it to him, they took my fingerprints. That was the end of due process. They decided the stockade was where I belonged. I spent the remainder of the afternoon sitting on a bare mattress waiting for chow.

It wasn't jambalaya, and the only exotic sauces offered were catsup and mustard, but it was plentiful, whatever it was. The armed forces have changed since my day. They seem to be accepting Boy Scouts, even though some of the young men looked as if their camp-out had been rained on.

Except for me, only one of the men in the dining hall was over thirty. He filled one side of a mess table all by himself, something like a basking sea lion. The food hadn't struck me as all that remarkable, but he was shoveling it in as if Julia Child did the catering. Unlike the other diners, he seemed happy. I took my tray over to join him.

"Looey," I said, "Arnie Buttons wants to know where you are."

He didn't stop chewing. "Thass tough," he said. "They frisked you, so get lost, shortie."

"I'm not going to be here long," I told him. "I got in by making them think I was AWOL. When

I get out tomorrow, people will be coming to see you. He's putting up a lot of money to lower your shades."

Looey finished his tray and looked at mine as he continued to chew. I passed it over and took a medicinal sip of something similar to coffee as he vacuumed up my supper.

"Whass he got on you?" he asked. "You're Frisbee, state attorney's office, right?"

I confessed my career change and my new assignment.

"A broad as hostage? Arnie's good at that. Well, like I always say, win some, lose some. Take me. They say I got something germinal. Six weeks or six months at the best to go. I can't remember which, so thass bad. But I been on a diet all my life. Now I eat as much as I want, no worries about hypertension or nothing. Arnie pro'ly can't tag me here, and all my tapes and depositions are going to stick it in his ear good. I go, and he follows. On the whole, thass good. You tell him for me."

I wondered how Arnie was going to take the news that modern medical science was going to achieve what he couldn't.

"Looey," I said, preparing to become persuasive, "Arnie tells me you're the only witness left. The others are missing or forgetful. They'll put you in a civilian hospital at the end. Then Arnie will do his number on your deathbed. After all, he found you here."

Looey's eyes were tiny slits in his enormous face. "I got this plan. I hit four hundred pounds, real sick, they won't move me out of here because they can't. In the meantime, I catch television and eat and think about Arnie sweating. Too bad about your broad."

In a lot of ways, Looey Flowers resembled a sea slug. The only place he was vulnerable was in his hatred of Arnie. Just as he was telling me he was maybe ninety percent sure his evidence would send Arnie down, I interrupted.

"I can make it one hundred percent."

He stopped eating to ask how.

My fingerprints came back from Washington the next morning. The provost marshal was pretty vexed when he discovered I hadn't been a member of the armed forces for some time. He felt better when he saw I had a right to the decorations. I said I was free-lancing what would be a very positive article about the efficiency of the local military police. Then I made a careful note of the way he spelled his name.

Arnie, on the other hand, wanted to be sure I knew he was mad. "You weren't supposed to lose Schmettler!"

"He lost me. He didn't want to go off with the air police. I did find Looey, though."

Arnie's sudden laugh wasn't reassuring, and neither was the golf bag in the back seat, large, with many zippered compartments. He handed me a briefcase that was indeed full of dirty money—old bills, all tens and twenties. I didn't like thinking where they came from.

"Now, let's go see Looey," he said, a tic jumping around his face.

"First, the call to Glendora," I told him. "Just to make sure, I'll use the pay phone on the corner."

Arnie shook his head no. Schmettler put his hand on my shoulder like a jail door slamming while Arnie explained.

"You call from the phone in the car, and I listen to every word. You're supposed to be tricky, and I'm taking no chances."

The black limousine was parked in a tow-away zone, but no tickets fluttered under the windshield wipers. I got in back while Schmettler locked all the interior doors from the driver's seat. The locks were child- and people-proof, which was not reassuring. Schmettler started up and Arnie handed over the phone. "No tricks, Frisbee."

"I found Looey and I've played all my tricks already," I said. Glendora came on immediately, and I felt better. I was sure she'd set up a phone trace. I can always count on her to show initiative.

"I found him, right where I thought he'd be," I said.

"And I'm still here," she said coolly. I had a sudden feeling something was very wrong. Arnie was connected everywhere, maybe even in the YWCA.

"What was I going to fix for supper last night?" I asked. If anything wasn't right, she'd give me a wrong answer.

"Jambalaya," she said and broke the connection.

Arnie inspected his fingernails. "We told her to hang up quick because you might have some idea of having the call traced. You're playing in the traffic again, Frisbee. You took dirty money to finger Looey Flowers. Where is he?"

Glendora was safe, so I told him. As Schmettler moved us back to the military reservation rapidly, Arnie began unzipping the golf bag. He was ready for anything—pistols, a carbine, a deer rifle, and what looked like a rocket launcher next to a machine pistol. There were even a couple of grenades. Arnie rubbed his jaw as he contemplated his armory. "Where's his cell?"

"I don't know, but he has the exercise yard all to himself from two till three every afternoon."

I went over my plan as we drove out to the brick buildings on the edge of the reservation where military delinquents put in hard time. About eighty yards off the roadway, his face a pale blob in the afternoon sun, a huge man leaned against the wall holding an orange Frisbee across his chest like a target. Even though it wasn't necessary, I pointed. "Looey Flowers. That takes care of my part of this."

Schmettler glanced at me through the mirror. I was the last pork chop on the plate. Arnie took my arm for emphasis. "That's a dummy stuffed with pillows."

Looey did look like a dummy, a fat scarecrow. "You're right," I said. "But I told you he had a serious weight problem. It's an effort for him just to breathe. Look, he moved."

Looey had dropped the Frisbee.

Arnie had reached the heights of his organization by being careful, which I had counted on. He told Schmettler to drive on.

"Frisbee," he announced, "I don't like not having a string on somebody who works for me, which is what you're doing from now on. We're going to shoot that loudmouth into pieces. But before we shoot, you shoot. That way, you're using a firearm during the commission of a felony, as guilty as we are."

I didn't have to search my memories of first-year law school to know he was right. I figured if Arnie didn't want a handle on me, I'd be dead by now, so I was glad he wanted a longer relationship.

After our stop at a turnaround for final instructions, we came back for the money run. Looey still looked like a sloppy bundle of clothes, just as I'd planned. After the fireworks, Arnie and Bruno would be arrested on the spot for all sorts of gun-law crimes and attempted murder. Since I wasn't a policeman, I hadn't entrapped them. Also, I wouldn't have compromised my pacifist principles. The plan was complicated, but it was working nicely.

The dummy leaned against the brick wall as if looking at cloud formations to the west. Schmettler readied the rocket launcher while Arnie nudged me out with his machine pistol. His instructions when he gave me the deer rifle were clear.

"You fire one round. Otherwise, we leave you here. To make sure, we don't fire till you do. Fire within the next five seconds or you get the first pill."

I drew a bead on a ventilation pipe sticking out the roof and squeezed off. Then the noise commenced. Arnie emptied a magazine into the target and nodded to Schmettler, who took his time and fired the rocket. There was *whoosh* and a giant slam! A hole appeared in the wall where the dummy had been leaning. Arnie took the deer rifle from me. I noticed he was wearing gloves.

About this time, a sufficient number of police of various jurisdictions were scheduled to rise out of the weeds and solve all my problems.

But nothing happened.

We drove off in silence. I missed the company of the law-enforcement types, but that wasn't the worst of it. Just as I'd put a hole in the steel ventilator, the dummy had raised an arm to make an international gesture at us.

I'd earned ten thousand the hard way. Looey Flowers was dead and Arnie had a hook in me. Things were very bleak indeed. I wondered how Arnie expected to get away with all that shooting, even on a military reservation. We drove back to the scenic turnout. As we parked, Arnie carefully put the deer rifle on the back seat, along with the rocket launcher and the machine pistol.

"We leave the guns here, especially the rifle with your prints on it."

We got out of the car and Schmettler started waving his tent-sized coat. Then I heard the *flat! flat! flat!* of a helicopter coming in. I felt really bad when Arnie punched my biceps.

"Sweet, hey? I reported the car stolen this morning right after your call. Us? When all this happened, we were riding over scenic Lake Pontchartrain in a helicopter you rented. The wise money will know what happened, but our story is Bruno and me flew down here to pick you up. You need me now, Frisbee."

I felt an unimprovable fool. I build a trap like the Taj Mahal and then put my own foot in it. Before I could feel sorry for myself, a loud hailer came on from overhead.

"Don't move! Federal agents! You're under arrest!"

Two other helicopters were coming up from other points of the compass. It was about time. Arnie started to break for the car, but I caught his collar and slammed him down. While I reached in to get the money, Schmettler looked at me, waiting for advice from Arnie.

I kept my foot on Arnie's neck while I explained things. "Bruno! Listen hard! You tell people Arnie hired you to kill Looey Flowers. If you turn state's evidence, you're safe. If you don't, it'll be Old Sparkie. Plus, for a limited time only, I give you this ten grand, tax-free."

As soon as the first chopper landed, I let Arnie up. He watched in disgust as Schmettler, his pockets stuffed with money, started telling his story to the first uniformed person who walked up.

"I want my lawyer!" Arnie shouted, but without much conviction. When Glendora got out of the last bird, he turned purple.

"There was no way you could get a message to that broad. What's she doing here? You didn't tell her a thing on the phone!"

Glendora was on the arm of Ralph David Luna, the special agent from the Plaquemines District across the river, a handsome devil with silver hair and a great tan. Arnie was being a bad loser. "There was no way you could trace that call!"

Glendora gave me an I'll-get-around-to-you-in-a-minute wave as she turned to Arnie. "We didn't have to trace calls, Mr. Buttons. As soon as my beau here told me Mr. Flowers had avoided a solid cordon of your people who were watching every possible exit on the base, I knew where he was."

If Arnie had turned purple when he saw Glendora, he was puce now. She took pity on him.

"Mr. Frisbee told me to listen carefully. He made quite a point that Looey had avoided your men. In law, evade and avoid are two different things. Tax evasion, for example, is a crime, but tax avoidance is not. That was the first clue. Since it wasn't against the law, that meant the forces of law were helping Mr. Flowers. The second clue was he said he'd see me today, and he's doing that. So it had to be someplace close. The base was close, so all I had left to do was work out where Mr. Flowers belonged. He belonged in jail. So he had to be in the base stockade."

Arnie turned to me. "You told her?"

Glendora explained further. "If Mr. Flowers had evaded your people, he'd have gone through them. But he avoided them by not leaving the base. Since he was in the stockade, they didn't need those marshals anymore. I figured Mr. Frisbee intended to bring you out here for reasons of his own. So we got in touch with the military and they told us the whole plan."

After they led Arnie away, she patted the cheek of the special agent from Plaquemines and nodded at the two large men in business suits who were still holding me. "He did a good job for us, you can let him go now."

"All right, Glendora," I told her.

"Why didn't I have them arrest you all at the scene of the crime? Well, Mr. Buttons sent a horrible woman to the YWCA to kill me. I decided if he was going to be like that, he couldn't be trusted not to kill *you*, so we decided to catch him with the helicopter he was expecting."

If she wanted me to interrupt and ask how she'd disposed of the threat in the YWCA, I wasn't going to cooperate, so I stood there pouting.

"You look real nice in blue," she said. "Anyway, after your call, I explained things to this nice Mr. Luna. When I told him for all intents I'd been kidnapped and left to languish in the YWCA, he saw the federal component right away. Especially after that call to the FBI about your fingerprints. So, this morning, we talked to Mr. Flowers, and he told us what you had in mind. They liked your idea of using a dummy, but then I guess Mr. Flowers thought it would be a real good joke all around if he stayed there. He had his first bad attack last night."

"The helicopter," I said.

"You must think that deep down I'm just a rattle-brain. When Mr. Buttons reported his car stolen, we knew he was going to use it for the crime and he'd need another way off the military reservation. So we checked all the heliports and, sure enough, he'd chartered a whirlybird in your name. So we decided to give him a real surprise. That way, he wouldn't try to shoot you with all those awful guns he had."

I finally got my serious question out. "Why'd you pat Luna's cheek?"

There came one of Glendora's super smiles guaranteed to make everything all right. "Why, I do believe you're jealous! Mr. Luna said after I finish law school, he'd like me to join the FBI. I told him I have other plans."

I'm sure she does, but I've been afraid to ask what they are.

Mean to My Father

CAROLYN BANKS

Carolyn Banks teaches creative writing at Austin Community College in Austin, Texas. Her fourth suspense novel, Patchwork, *was published by Crown in spring 1986, and her previous novel,* The Girls on the Row, *was recently reprinted in paperback by Fawcett-Crest. She is presently indulging her interest in horses, working on a nonfiction book for Texas Monthly Press tentatively titled* The Horse Lover's Guide to Texas.

MY MOTHER and my aunt say that I was mean to my father. At least, they used to say it when he was alive. They said that whenever he put his arms around me, I would make a face and pull away, and then he would feel sad.

And that's true.

I never meant to be that way. I always promised myself that the next time he came to me, I would hug him back. Maybe even kiss him on the cheek.

But then he would be there and I could smell his breath and see the red veins on his nose and something inside me would twist up. It was like what the nuns in school called a reflex, except that when they talked about it, it had to do with knees. You hit your knee and it would jerk away, even if you didn't want it to. Well, that's the way I was about my father.

My mother and my aunt said I was a cold fish, and I guess they were right.

I wasn't always like that, though, except that I used to go down in the cellar sometimes and sit all by myself. When I was real little. I guess, if you think about it, that was a sign.

I would sit behind the cabinet where my mother kept cans of soup and stuff and smell the smell of bleach and ammonia. She only did the wash on Saturdays, but it smelled that way all the time. It smelled clean.

And it looked clean, too. We had a coal bin down there for the furnace, but you couldn't really tell over on the side where I used to sit. The walls had been whitewashed and they were bright-white, because once a week my mother took a broom and swept the soot off the walls, swept them the way she did the floors. I made that part of the cellar my thinking place.

Not that I was that much of a thinker. The nuns in school were always yelling at me, and they would hit me, too, with a ruler across the palms of my hands. The only good thing about school was Nancy Killian, who was my friend.

At least, she was my friend in third grade, when she

came to our school. And in fourth. The first part of fourth. Around the middle of fourth, she died.

She didn't just die. She was stabbed thirteen times. They said her brother did it and he was sent away, but not to jail. To a hospital. But they said he would never get out and, as far as I know, he never did.

Nancy Killian was just like me. She wanted to work in an office when she grew up, just like me. She wanted a puppy and her mother wouldn't let her have one, just like me. Except that she had a brother, a brother who was home all the time or else at the river, down by the trains. Or hanging out at the store where the pinball machine was. She had a bum for a brother, that's what my mother said.

Nancy Killian didn't come to school the day she was stabbed. She had a fight with me the day before and she ripped half of the hem out of my dress. And I said I would never talk to her again, never, and went home.

But my mother yelled at me about my dress and told me money didn't grow on trees and that decent little girls didn't go around fighting. I went down in the cellar to my thinking place and wished that I could be friends with Nancy again.

I was going to make up with her at school the next day, the day she didn't show up. The day she was stabbed.

Most of the kids ate lunch at school every day because their mothers, like my mother and Nancy Killian's, worked at the linoleum factory down the street. And their fathers worked, too, the way mine did and hers did, in gray shirts and gray pants, and big, heavy shoes. But my aunt lived up the street from Nancy's house and she would make me soup for lunch, so I was allowed to go there.

I went to Nancy's house first, though. I knocked on the back door and I went around to the front door and knocked there, too, even though we weren't allowed to come in that way. But Nancy didn't come. And then I felt as though Nancy was mad at me forever and we would never be friends again.

So I went home just to be sad instead of going to my aunt's house to eat. And I went to my thinking place and I thought, not just about Nancy, but about how mad my aunt was going to be that I didn't go there for lunch and what the nuns would say and my mother.

I heard the cellar door come open and I saw the bottoms of my father's legs on the top step. Then he came down and I watched him, more of his legs and more and then all of him.

"Oh," I said out loud. His shirt and his pants had blood on them. Not bright red, but darker. Still, blood. And I went over and even grabbed his hand. I wasn't mean to my father then. But his hand was bloody, too.

I asked him if he got hurt at work and he said yes. And then he told me to go upstairs and get ready to go back to school. That he wouldn't tell my mother I was there if I didn't tell her he got hurt at work. And I said okay.

When I went up the steps I saw him taking clean work clothes off the line that my mother had hung in the basement. And then I heard him running the water into the laundry tub. And then I heard the big roar that the furnace makes when somebody opens the door and the whole cellar turns orange.

And after that, everything was different. Nancy Killian never came back to school and the newspapers had her picture in it almost every day for over a week. And her brother got sent away, like I said. And I started being mean to my father.

Killer's Mind

MICHAEL COLLINS

"Killer's Mind" is the second appearance by Michael Collins' detective Dan Fortune in New Black Mask. This story is another in his series of fictional experiments; here he combines the puzzle story and hard-boiled forms. Mr. Collins, who considers himself basically a short-story writer, says that it is his intention to use mystery stories for a purpose uncommon to them.

WE HAD AN HOUR before they brought the woman to Captain Pearce's office, went over the whole scheme. Pearce himself, Lieutenant Schatz from the precinct, and me. The captain had an open mind, Schatz didn't. Schatz doesn't like theories, and he doesn't like private detectives because they have too many theories.

Pearce said, "Castro planned to kill Roth from the start?"

"It was all that made sense."

Schatz made a noise. "You've got no proof Castro planned anything, Fortune. How about some facts?"

"All right," I said. "Fact one: Three years ago Roth was Castro's junior partner. Almost overnight Roth had a big contract that should have been Castro's, was in business for himself, had stolen Castro's wife, and Castro hated him."

Schatz shook his head. "Three years is too long to wait."

"Castro didn't wait," I said. "That's fact number two—when I started investigating the killing I found out Castro had been working hard to ruin Roth's business as soon as he realized what Roth had done to him."

"But murder?" Pearce said. "After three years? In hot blood, maybe. But Schatz's right, a smart, educated man like Castro should have cooled down by then."

"Revenge," I said, "and his ex-wife back, and his sons."

"You think he really figured the wife would go back to him after he murdered Roth?" Schatz said.

"Yes," I said. "She's a practical woman."

Schatz shook his head. "Theory, Fortune, and crazy theory."

"Theory," I agreed, "but all I had. No clues, no evidence, no real facts. From the start I didn't have a damn thing to go on except the theory and my imagination."

From the moment the company hired me—Dan Fortune, Private Investigator—I had nothing to work with except a hunch about Maxwell Castro. No facts, no evidence. Nowhere even to start to prove it all, except to get inside Maxwell Castro's mind. Try to think the way Castro had thought. Become Max Castro—successful architect and bitter man—wrestling with his hate . . .

He had to kill Norman Roth.

If he was to get his wife back, keep his sons, it had to be murder. There was no other way, not any longer.

He understood his ex-wife. In the end she'd go to the winner. A practical woman. Three years ago it had been Norman Roth, the sure winner. So she had divorced him and married Roth. It was what she would always do.

"You were good for me, Max, but Norman's going to be better." Susan had smiled. "You're getting old. Why should I settle for an old rich man when I can have a young rich man?"

He'd wanted to kill the son of a bitch right then, but three years ago murder was too big a risk. He'd be the first suspect. There were safer ways then to stop Norman Roth, get Susan back.

Susan was a woman who shaped her present and her future. He'd always admired that, knew it was the reason she'd married him in the first place. A lot of men had wanted her, and he'd been no more than a small architect getting near middle age in a large firm. It was Susan who had convinced him to strike out on his own, used her contacts to help him, pushed him relentlessly.

It made him proud even now to realize that Susan had expected him to succeed from the beginning. He had been the winner she had to have, each partnership bigger than the last. He smiled as he remembered his climb over partner after partner to build one of the largest architectural firms in the city, the state, maybe the whole damned country.

Until he had taken on Norman Roth as his junior partner.

Young, handsome, Norman Roth! Outsmarted by a cheap stud like Roth! That was almost worse than losing his wife and sons, worse than the loss of the Shea contract itself. To be beaten by a fucking pretty boy not even thirty years old!

Castro tossed sleepless in his solitary bed in the large, empty apartment when he thought of that moment three years ago when Norman Roth had his contract and his wife. Of two years ago when Norman Roth, Architects, had more business than Castro & Sons. Of . . .

The frustration, rage squirmed through Max Castro's mind. The rage and defeat inside the mind of a man accustomed to success. A man who knew he was superior. A different breed from normal men. I sensed that rage, that frustration. Felt it inside me as I put myself in his place from the start.

Captain Pearce studied the copy of my report to the company. It detailed Maxwell Castro's actions over the last two-plus years.

"So Castro took hold of himself," I said, "began his fight to destroy Roth. A good architect and a super businessman, he worked hard, took big financial risks. He worked for almost no profit just to get contracts. For a time he actually lost money, but he almost had Roth beaten, on the ropes."

Schatz said, "So why suddenly switch to murder? It doesn't make any damn sense, Fortune."

"His sons," I said. "About three months ago his ex-wife called him, suggested he take her out to lunch. She had a real surprise for Castro."

I saw her, too, the woman. Susan Roth, once Susan Castro. She was young, beautiful. Sat there across the white linen and silver of Max Castro's table in the exclusive lunch club after almost three years. Castro looked at the woman he still wanted, who had called so unexpectedly, who smiled at him. I imagined Castro smiling back. . . .

"Face it, Susan, you made a mistake. Maybe the first mistake of your life. Admit it, come back where you belong."

The almost soundless waiter brought their drinks. Her martini with a dash of *fino* sherry, his beer: Sierra Nevada Ale brought from the Coast just for him. She sipped her martini.

"I don't make mistakes, Maxwell," Susan said. "If you did ruin Norman, I probably would come back to you. I admit it because it won't happen. I never back a loser, you know that."

"We all make mistakes, Susan," Max Castro said.

"I don't," Susan said. "You're a winner, Max, up to a point. Norman's going to be a bigger winner." She sipped. "He's younger, more exciting, a lot better in bed. You're all you're ever going to be, Max. It's not enough. I want more."

Castro wanted to hit her right there in the hushed club with its immaculate whites and silvers. Tear her clothes off, show her how wrong she was, but his mind became wary. Did she know something that he didn't know?

She said, "But I didn't come to talk about me. I came to talk about the boys."

"The boys?"

"Norman wants them to be ours, Max, you understand?"

He stared at her. Understand? Understand what?

"We've started proceedings to legally adopt them. You'll be notified in a day or so, but I thought perhaps we could agree on it amicably. Why give the lawyers money?"

"Adoption?"

His mind seemed to be a block of ice. The boys?

"They would, of course, take Norman's name."

Her voice came from across a vast distance, a glacier, the empty Antarctic. *His* sons! Named Roth? *Roth!* The sons of Maxwell Castro to be named *Roth!*

"Never! You hear! Never!"

"I'd really rather not fight about it, Maxwell. But—?"

The *maître* turned to look at them. Castro took a deep breath. No court would let a stepfather take children away from the natural father without his consent.

It was another trick of hers. He waved for a new bottle of his ale.

"It won't work, Susan," Castro said. "I'm going to ruin your playboy genius. You can't blackmail me with the boys. No court would go against the natural father, and that's me. In case you don't remember where the boys came from."

Max Castro grinned at his ex-wife. She didn't grin.

"The court will back us up, Max," Susan said, "but I'd rather stay out of court. The boys are so very young. They'll probably have half brothers soon. They already wonder why they have one name and we have another. We'd really like your consent."

Stunned as he was, he smiled and tried to hide his turmoil and fury behind some light sarcasm. "My consent? Yes, I expect you would like that. Make it all a lot easier, eh?"

"It would, Maxwell. Especially for the boys."

He nodded, looked serious. "A court battle would be very hard on them at their age."

"Then you will sign the papers?" Susan said, just a little too quickly. "Give Norman the boys? Let them take his name?"

His name! The rage welled up inside him again. He fought hard to keep it down, hide it. Pretended to consider the impossible idea while inside he boiled. First his contract. Then his wife and his boys. Now his name!

"I'll consider it, Susan." He would not consider it. His mind could not even begin to consider it. But he needed time. He needed to have her think he would, in the end, agree.

"Norman can give them much more than you ever will. You must know that by now."

It was the breaking point. He began to shout in the elegant club, his ale forgotten. The other elite diners turned to look.

"My sons are mine, you hear? I'll never consent, and no court will take them away from me!"

The *maître* hurried over. Could he help monsieur? The other diners, monsieur. Max Castro sat pale, his fine, honey-like ale forgotten. Susan drank her martini, looked past him.

"The court will back us, Maxwell," she said, her voice soft, almost gentle. "Norman has the best lawyers, influence in the city. We'll prove you're an unfit father. A child-beater. Even a child molester. We have witnesses. You remember that maid you fired? Josie? Those baby-sitters you threw out of the apartment for smoking pot? There's my mother, my sister. Then the boys themselves. The way you gave them baths, dressed them. Innocent, but when we coach the boys—"

Max Castro sat in the fine club with its white cloth and crystal glasses, shining silver and dark-green walls, the silent waiters. He had always loved to eat lunch here, the elegance of it, the privilege, the power. Now he barely knew where he was. Her voice soft as a snake gliding into his ears.

"I can do it, Maxwell. You know me. Think how horrible for the boys. For you."

He would die and his business would go to his boys, and then Roth would have his business too. They would have it all. He had to fight. But would he win? If she told the court he . . . If witnesses said he . . . molested . . . battered . . .

Susan stood up. "You really have no choice, Maxwell. We'll get the boys in the end, with or without you."

Maxwell Castro sat in the lunch club long after his ex-wife had left, a taste of ashes in his mouth. His *sons!* She was so sure. His stomach was tight, painful. Sure of her lying scheme to steal the boys from him, and of what else? What had happened, or was going to happen, to make Susan so confident?

He went to work, checked all his information sources. It took three days, and then the reports came to him. Roth wasn't ruined. His campaign had failed. Roth was not only unhurt, he was moving upward again. Bigger and better contracts. Roth would succeed, and Roth would get his sons.

No.

Norman Roth would *not* get Maxwell Castro's sons. This time Susan was definitely wrong. He had a choice. A very clear and obvious choice. He would kill Norman Roth.

I heard Max Castro's inner voice. He would kill Norman Roth as he had really wanted to from the first moment Roth had stolen the Shea contract and Susan. A voice of hate, of fury, of panic at the loss of everything that belonged to him, that whispered over and over in his mind: Kill Norman Roth! Kill Norman Roth!

We still had half an hour before the woman would be brought into Pearce's office.

"Castro named his company Castro & Sons as soon as his second boy was born," I said. "The adoption threat did it. And the failure of his plan to ruin Roth. I located the confidential reports Castro got after Susan Roth's visit. Roth had been awarded the big Haskins Urban Redevelopment Project contract. General architect, the works. It would save Roth and a lot more. Roth had floated a large loan, had already advanced money to a lot of suppliers. Roth was safe, moving ahead again. With Susan's lies, witnesses, he would get Castro's sons."

Lieutenant Schatz wasn't convinced, paced the office behind its drawn shades. "Okay, he had a motive. But he had to have known he'd be the first man we'd suspect. We'd be down on him before Roth got cold, Fortune. He'd have to have been crazy."

"Most killers are crazy," I said. "But Castro knew he'd be the first suspect. He planned it with that in mind."

I tried to plan it exactly as Maxwell Castro had, our minds a single mind. The pattern was clear as I thought it out with Castro. Alone in his office, smoking cigarette after cigarette, he worked it all out as he would have worked out some delicate problem in architecture. Careful. Logical . . .

Max Castro knew that damn few premeditated murderers went uncaught. It was a fact, and it was *why* murderers were caught—*because they knew that murderers were almost always caught!*

The killer planned, complicated, made an intricate scheme to turn away any shadow of guilt. All possible dangers prevented, all possible suspicion diverted.

Attempted to hide his homicide by disguising it as something else. An accident. A senseless killing by some insane night prowler. The panic murder of a startled burglar. Sometimes he worked out a crazy plan to make the murder look like death from natural causes, relied on a shaky verdict of suicide.

He beat his brains out to hide his motive. He planned on an unsolved murder! The police would give up in the face of his cleverness, file the crime away to gather dust and be forgotten.

Or, the most certain of all to fail, the killer laid false trails that would be sure to lead the police to someone else, but that, in the end, always led to him.

The killer, aware of danger, planned a crime so intricate and complicated, it was all but inevitable he would be caught.

He, Castro, would not do that.

What a killer could devise, the police could detect. What one man could hide, another man could find. Max Castro would hide nothing.

The answer was simplicity. Exactly like the clean, simple lines of a modern building. A simple line for a building, a simple plan for a murder. An obvious murder. A murder that pointed straight to only one murderer. Himself.

Because it isn't enough for the police to know that a man committed murder. They have to prove it. Not that he had wanted to commit murder, but that he had committed murder.

He, Castro, would be the logical suspect. He would have no alibi. Definitely no alibi.

The stupid, iron-clad alibi. Stupid, because no alibi could be iron-clad since it was, in fact, an alibi, and not the truth. It was a lie, something that had *not* happened. The smallest unexpected accident, and the alibi was broken. And once broken, the alibi itself, the carefully constructed lie, became the most damning evidence against the killer.

No, when Norman Roth was dead, the police would come straight to him, Castro. He would say, "Yes, officer, I often thought of killing him myself. I'm glad he's dead. As a matter of fact, I was very near where he was killed at just the time it happened. It's my normal routine to walk past there at that time. I certainly could have killed him, but I didn't. Can you prove that I did?"

Finally, he would not confess. That last and most fatal flaw in any killer's plan. The weakness of guilt that made a man break down under pressure.

Castro would feel no guilt at all. Not for killing one thieving son-of-bitch young stud.

He would not break under questioning.

He was a man of position and wealth.

He could protect himself.

And he would not be forced to confess to save an innocent person. He would be the only real suspect. Susan would have an alibi, a real alibi, and the scene would be completely deserted.

Castro, thought, planned. . . .

*In Castro's mind I felt his excitement as his plan took
its final, utterly simple shape. The last little thought—
the old criminal adage: If you are innocent, always
take a judge alone for your trial. If you are guilty, take
a jury. A carefully selected jury, a reasonable doubt, no
proof, and a good lawyer.*

Captain Pearce chewed on his lip. "So he just walked
up to Roth as bold as you please?"

"It has to be," I said. "I've studied his actions, put
myself into his mind. There's no other answer."

Lieutenant Schatz swore in the smoky office. "No
fingerprints, no usable footprints, no bloodstains, no
hair or skin under the fingernails, nothing dropped, no
physical evidence at all. A thousand other bricks just
like the murder weapon all over that building site.
Castro walked past the place at that time every Mon-
day, Thursday, and Friday for months."

"All part of his plan," I said. "Those were the days
Susan Roth had her alibi. Thursday, the day it happened, was her usual Junior League meeting."

Pearce shook his head. "And Castro planned it all,
Dan?"

"Every detail," I said. "As simple as he could make
it. Just walked onto that deserted building site and
straight up to Norman Roth inside the shell of the
unfinished building where no one could see them
together."

*The perfect place—I heard Castro thinking it. I walked
with Castro past the building site of Roth's new job.
He couldn't have selected a better site if he had gone*

168

to Roth and told the bastard just what he needed for a simple murder. And Roth, good at his work, made a point of visiting his various building sites after the day's work was finished. As Castro knew he did. After all, it was Castro who had taught the younger man always to do just that. You never knew what would pay off in the end.

He watched and waited. The building site was in a downtown business area deserted after six o'clock. It was hidden from view on three sides. The foundation was already in, the walls just rising.

He began to walk from his office to his own site by way of Roth's building. He bought a newspaper at the same stand each day. People would remember him, yet would not really notice him.

Who really notices a plainly dressed man on a city street in the evening twilight day after day? Who actually remembers the precise time they saw the man if he strolls often along that same city street? They would remember that he walked that way regularly, but would forget the exact day or time when they had last seen him. Was it Wednesday or Thursday? Perhaps Friday?

He chose a drugstore not far from Roth's building site and stopped there regularly for a soda. The same each time, and talked to the boy behind the counter.

"You make a very good cherry soda, son."

The boy grinned. "Thank you, sir."

"Castro," he smiled. "Max Castro. You look like a smart kid. Too smart to be working behind a soda fountain. You should better yourself. Ever consider architecture?"

"Yessir, I sure have!" the boy said eagerly. "Architecture's what I want to study in college when I get enough money."

Every murderer needs a little luck.

"Good," he said. "It happens to be my profession. I'm on my way to one of my buildings now. An ex-partner of mine, Norman Roth, has a building going up only a few blocks away. I stop there too, to see how I'd do it better."

He laughed at his own joke, hinted some help might be arranged for the boy, and tipped too much.

"Thank *you*, sir!"

He made small purchases, browsed among the paper-back books and magazines. The browsing was so that the owner of the store would also remember him, and the small purchases did two things. First, they involved him more in the store, increased the chance of being recalled as a regular by customers. Second, they helped his innocent appearance. Who buys a bottle of aspirin or a tube of toothpaste on his way to commit murder?

He talked to the boy about Norman Roth. "You go and look at Roth's building, son. Three blocks straight up on this side of the street. His name is on the sign. He's not much of an architect, but he's a publicity whiz."

He talked a lot about Norman Roth. That would look good. Why would a man who planned to kill talk so much about his intended victim to a stranger who would be sure to remember?

He even brought the boy some books. "Read them, they'll help you with the mathematics, help you understand architects and architecture, feel the pull."

"I was always real good at math," the boy said.

"That'll help a lot," he encouraged.

At the actual building site he stopped whenever Roth himself was there. The workmen and Roth's associates noticed him. He made sure they saw him and Roth together, talking.

"Go away, Castro," Roth said. "Anything you have to say to me you can say in court."

"I like to study your cheap work." Castro smiled.

"Stay away from me, you hear? You can't hurt me. You're a loser, Castro. Work and women."

"I walk where I please," Castro said, but inside his teeth clenched, and he could barely hold himself from attacking Roth then and there in front of everyone.

He continued his routine, made sure he passed the site just at twilight. Sometimes Roth was there, sometimes he wasn't. Usually he had to wait for Roth to drive up from one of his other sites. Roth wasn't always alone. But most of the time he was.

Twice in July Roth was alone at the site in the late twilight. The first time a group of young boys would not leave the site even when Roth himself tried to chase them away, swore at them in fury as they defied him.

The second time Castro was sure it was the moment. As he walked up the empty street, Roth was alone. The younger man went inside the unfinished shell out of sight from the street. Castro moved quickly to the opening without a door. He bent to pick up the brick. Roth suddenly came out of the building again.

Roth was too young, too big. Castro couldn't attack when Roth was facing him. So he smiled, talked to Roth casually as he had done before, then walked away along the street as usual.

His heart pounded, and his head throbbed. But he calmed himself again. He had to wait, be sure. . . .

I felt the blood pound in Max Castro's head, heard his voice tell himself he had to wait. In his killer's mind I heard him say it over and over: Wait . . . be patient. Haste, that was the greatest danger. Impatience. I heard his mind tell himself day after day: Slow, careful; don't panic, don't rush it; slow and careful and wait and there'll be no mistakes. . . .

All the weeks I'd spent digging, checking Castro's routine and route past Norman Roth's building, were on Captain Pearce's desk.

"He could have gone along other streets," I said. "He could have driven. But he was a known walker, and the route was logical enough. Stopping at that drugstore became a routine. He talked to Roth whenever Roth was at the site, casual and hiding nothing."

Pearce nodded. "They all remember seeing him often."

"But not one damned person is sure they saw him the day of the killing," Schatz said.

"He planned it just that way," I said.

"He walked right onto that building site and straight up to Roth," Pearce said. "And no one saw anything."

Schatz swore again. "A reasonable doubt all the way. Any jury would buy it."

I felt Castro's mind that last day. Eager, the adrenaline pumping. Time pressed in on him. The day had to come soon. Would it be that day? He couldn't hold himself back much longer, the adoption proceedings would be before the judge soon. I felt the thin thread of tension, his mind fighting . . . go slow . . . follow the routine. . . .

He dressed for the twentieth, thirtieth, *nth* time in the cheap suit, checked the buttons again to be sure they were on tight. His fingernails had been cut and filed to the quick for months. He left all his jewelry in his office once more. His hair had been washed every day, all the labels had been removed from his clothes long ago. He carried nothing on his walk past Roth's site that could be dropped, not even his cigarettes or matches.

In the drugstore he browsed, bought a new razor, had his cherry ice-cream soda. He talked to the counter boy about the books he had lent the boy. That, he thought, was an especially good touch. A smart lawyer could make a lot of the books, with his nameplate in the front, as a sure sign that he couldn't have been planning a murder that day.

A noisy group of juveniles slouched into the store

and engaged the counter boy with multiple orders. He was held up a few minutes, with dusk settling outside. He didn't think it would be serious, Roth always remained at the site at least five minutes to make his inspection, usually longer, but he decided not to stop and talk to the owner this time as he paid his check.

On the street he walked a little bit faster. He bought his newspaper, spoke briefly to the newsstand man, and continued briskly on to the site. Fast, but not so fast as to attract any attention, and it was just dusk as he reached Roth's building.

The street was deserted as usual, the other buildings dark, the twilight gloomy, the site itself silent. He stood back in the shadows and waited. His plan had always been rigid: Walk away instantly if even possibly seen by anyone, and, if unseen, five minutes' wait and not a second more.

He had one minute to go when the car drove up. Norman Roth stepped out, seemed to search the twilight for a moment. Castro tensed, ready to follow the younger man into the empty building shell. Roth leaned back into the car to speak to someone.

The car was Susan's car! She was dropping Roth off on her way to her Thursday Junior League meeting. Not even Roth's car would be on the street to attract anyone's attention!

Roth leaned in for a kiss, turned and walked across the sidewalk and the dirt to his partly finished building.

Susan drove off around the next corner.

The street was empty.

It was at just that stage of dusk when it is harder to

see than in full night, and no one was in sight any-where.

Castro hurried across the debris of the building site. As he neared his enemy he slowed, became casual. He made a small smile play across his face. Roth heard him, turned.

"Don't you ever give up?" Roth said.

"No, Norman, never," Max Castro said.

"Go away, Castro. You're beaten," Norman Roth said. "I'm getting the boys, there isn't a fucking thing you can do."

With a gesture of contempt, Roth turned his back and walked into the interior of the unfinished building.

The hate surged through Max Castro. He looked around once more. He was totally alone in the dusk, all but invisible.

He bent, picked up the brick, stepped through the open doorway into the hidden interior of the unfinished building. He looked for Norman Roth, the brick raised.

Norman Roth struck viciously.

Pain hammered through Max Castro's head.

Something dusty, smothering, covered Castro.

The brick in Norman Roth's hand smashed . . . smashed. . . .

I felt the crushing pain as Norman Roth bludgeoned Max Castro with the brick. The shock, and the fear, and the horror, and the final agony of all—the moment of realization that he, Maxwell Castro, had, after all, lost. A loser. A dead man. The horrible agony as Castro realized he was not the hunter but the hunted. Not the predator but the prey. Outwitted. Dead. . . .

I sat in Captain Pearce's dim, silent office behind its drawn shades that seemed to make the city outside light-years away.

"It was the only way they could have gotten Castro to that building site under those conditions at that time. He would never have gone there alone, at dusk, unarmed, unprotected, unless *he* was planning to kill Roth."

"Theory, Fortune," Schatz said. "That's all you've got."

"It's the only answer," I said. "Castro set up the conditions, and Roth and his wife used them to murder him. They manipulated him like Pavlov's dog, goaded him until they were sure he would decide to kill Roth. That was *their* plan, and Castro walked into the trap like a sheep to the slaughter."

Pearce said, "Roth waited inside that building shell." His voice had a tone of wonder. "He hit Castro once with the brick, covered him with a canvas tarpaulin, and hit him four more times. No blood except under the canvas. No witnesses. No fingerprints on the brick or canvas. No clues. The debris on Roth from the building site is useless, he went there every day. Only not that day, he says, and we can't prove he did. No evidence at all."

"Except," I said, "Castro's little mistake."

Schatz shook his head in even more wonder. "Both of them, Castro and Roth, stripped of everything. No labels, no jewelry, no hair or skin under fingernails, nothing. Zero."

"Yeah," I said, "that's what got me thinking. Castro had nothing in his pockets—not even cigarettes, and he was a smoker. No labels. A cheap suit. Fingernails cut to the quick. With Castro the victim, those things made no sense. But if Castro had been the killer, then it made a lot of sense. So I put myself in his mind, dug into what had made him decide to commit murder. Then I did the same for Roth and the woman, imagined how they planned to make Castro try to kill Roth, how they rigged it."

I had been inside one killer's mind, Castro's, and now I put myself inside the minds of two killers. Saw the scene between them, Norman Roth and his wife. Susan Roth, once Susan Castro.

Norman Roth lay naked in the giant circular bed of the luxury condominium high above the city. Tall and muscular, lean in the hips, he looked up at himself in the mirrored ceiling of the bedroom. "He's going to beat me, Susan. He's a fucking devil in business. He's taking losses, cutting corners, ruining me."

"I like a winner, Norman," Susan Roth said.

"Susan!" Roth stared at her.

She was still slim, curved, her breasts reflected full in the ceiling mirror. She touched Roth in the bed. Her fingers played with his belly, stroked his chest.

"If he beats you, I'll go back to him," she said. "I can't live without what success brings, Norman. Big success. I never lied about that. I'm a practical woman, Norman."

"I'll never let him take you back!"

"Then stop him," Susan said.

"I've tried. I'm almost to the wall. The only way I can stop him now is to kill him."

"All right," Susan said. "Kill him."

Roth blinked at her. "Kill—?"

She kissed his neck, his throat. Her tongue flicked over his chest as she slid softly against his body.

"He'd kill you," Susan said. "But we'll kill him first."

"How can we kill him? The police would guess at once it was me. Or you. The way he's ruining me, ruining us."

"But they would have to prove it, Norman," Susan said, licked his belly. "We'll make it simple. We'll make Max come to you where there'll be only the two of you alone, and no evidence afterward, and they can't prove you were there when it happened."

"What in God's name would make Castro come to me like that?"

"To kill *you*," Susan Roth said simply.

Roth looked at her and at her naked body touching him in the big bed. "Why would he kill me? He's already got me ruined."

Her tongue was in his ear now, her breath. "We make him think you're not anywhere near ruined. We convince him you're growing bigger and richer every day, and then we make him have to murder you fast or lose something very important to him."

"Lose what?"

178

She kissed him, smiled down into his eyes. "The boys, Norman. We start proceedings to legally adopt the boys. *His* boys. We threaten to take his sons from him."

Roth stared, then began to laugh. "Castro & Sons!"

"It's the one thing that would make Max commit murder—the loss of Castro & Sons." Susan Roth smiled. "His sons with your name. His business with your name."

Roth laughed aloud. He grabbed her, rolled her over on the bed, kissed her breasts, kissed her mound, kissed . . . Stopped.

"The business! It won't work if he thinks he's ruining me, and he *is* ruining me."

Susan Roth stretched and looked up at their naked bodies in the mirrored ceiling. "You've been invited to bid on the Haskins Project. Make your bid so low they must give it to you. They don't reveal details of the bids."

Roth shook his head. "A bid low enough to be sure would lose me a fortune. We'd really be ruined, and for keeps."

"Not with Max dead," Susan said. "A calculated risk, Norman. With Max gone we would get his insurance, his money, and his business. Or the boys would, and that means me. We'd have it all, and you could absorb the Haskins loss."

"I'd need money up front to start the work, make it look good, and no one would give me a loan the way things are now."

"I have my jewels, some securities. We'll get a loan

with them as collateral. Maxwell won't know how we got the loan. He'll find you have the contract and the money, are going ahead bigger and better. He'll have to kill you. He's wanted to from the start. You took his contract, his wife, and his male ego. I've known that all along. Now we can use it to save ourselves."

"Will the courts let us adopt the boys without his consent?"

"They will if we can prove Max is an unfit father, a child molester, and we can. Or we'll make Max think we can, and that's all it will take. He wants to kill you, Norman. We'll give him a good excuse, make him tell himself there's no other way."

Roth stared at her, perhaps suddenly a little bit afraid of her. Afraid and excited too. They stared at each other in the giant bed high above the city, Maxwell Castro's ex-wife and his most hated enemy. They looked at each other with the excitement of victory and even of death, and that brought another kind of excitement. An excitement that isn't all that different.

Afterward they began to plan.

They set the business wheels in motion, Susan had her lunch with Max Castro. Then they made Castro wait and wait until he was on the verge of exploding with his hate. When they were ready, they decided on a Thursday, the night of Susan Roth's Junior League meeting.

"I've timed it, Norman," Susan said. "If I drive from the apartment to the Junior League faster than usual, or slower than usual, there is only a difference of five minutes in total time."

Roth nodded. "No jury would convict anyone on a

matter of five minutes in city traffic. Not without a lot of evidence."

"And there won't be any. As long as no one sees you with Maxwell at the site, we're safe, and Maxwell himself will make sure no one sees you, eh?"

They both laughed.

"Even if someone notices the car," Susan went on, "it will be just an unidentified car on a dark street for a few moments. It will be far too dark to read the license plate. They'll know we killed him, but they won't be able to prove it."

That Thursday, Roth volunteered to work at the Junior League himself. He told his men that he would not visit the site that night. He told them to knock off at the regular time.

Roth and Susan went to the empty site. She dropped him off. Castro waited. Roth killed him. Susan came back two minutes after Castro had arrived. A minute later Roth walked from the deserted building. Susan held the door open for him, he slipped into the car. Susan ran back around the car to the driver's seat, drove off. Roth looked at his watch.

"Four minutes flat."

They arrived at the Junior League exactly at Susan's usual time. Traffic had been a little lighter than normal. From the numbers, they couldn't have stopped anywhere.

As they worked at the Junior League, they smiled.

I sensed them still smiling when the police came the next morning. They were shocked, horrified, but admitted quite readily that they had hated Castro and were glad he was dead. They admitted they wanted him dead, but they certainly hadn't killed him. They defied the police to come up with a shred of evidence. They knew they had made no mistakes, not one.

In his office above the city, Captain Pearce sighed. "Not one mistake, Fortune. They're right. We've got no real evidence."

"No one else could have done it," I said.

"Or anyone else," Schatz said.

Pearce nodded. "A tramp, a drunk, a psycho, a scared kid caught trespassing by Castro. Some enemy of Castro's we don't even know exists. Roth's lawyer will make hash of a jury."

"Except for Castro's mistake," I said, "and the flaw in the Roths' plan."

Pearce was doubtful. "It's pretty thin, Dan."

"Thin and theory," Schatz said. "No DA is going to even go to a grand jury with what you've got, Fortune."

"He won't have to," I said.

They said nothing. They weren't exactly convinced. Neither was I, really, but what I had was all I was going to get as far as evidence was concerned. I hoped it would be enough. I was pretty certain it would be, but it had been a long, hard case and you never know for sure.

"It's funny," I said. "Castro had a perfect plan without a flaw, but he made a mistake. Roth and Susan Roth didn't make a single mistake, but their plan had one flaw—the alibi. They had to have an alibi." I shook my head. "Because their plan had a flaw, and Castro made a small mistake, they're going over."

How do you explain one small mistake? Castro's plan was literally foolproof—if he made no mistakes. What made that one careless moment? I was inside his mind and I didn't know. The waiting? The anxiety to get it done after all those weeks, months? Maybe it was, in the end, only fate, the roll of the dice, working on three lives that last Thursday....

The boy stood behind the soda fountain counter.

"Dead? Mr. Castro's dead?"

"Murdered," I said. "It was in all the newspapers."

"I don't read the papers. I'm studying to be an architect. I liked Mr. Castro."

"Two weeks ago Thursday," I said.

The boy blinked at me, frowned. "Two weeks? Thursday? Gee, maybe that's why I couldn't find him, you know? I mean, it was two weeks ago, sure. Thursday."

"Find him?" I said. "Two weeks ago?"

"He forgot the razor he bought," the boy explained. "We had some loud kids, you know, and he had to wait to pay for his cherry soda and the razor. He walked out fast, forgot to take the package. He was gone maybe three, four minutes when I saw it. The package, I mean. I told the boss, and he let me go after Mr. Castro with the razor. I mean—the boss, he liked Mr. Castro too. So the boss took over on the fountain and I went out and tried to catch up with Mr. Castro."

"You went after him two weeks ago Thursday?"

"I knew which way he always walked 'cause he talked to me a lot about going to visit this building of some guy named Roth about three blocks up. I figured he'd probably stop there and I could catch him. Only, when I got there, no one was around."

"You went to Roth's building five minutes after Castro left your store, but you didn't see anyone?"

"Not when I got there, and I never did see Mr. Castro. But when I was leaving I saw this big guy come out of the building and get into a car. It wasn't Mr. Castro, and there was only a woman in the car, so I walked back to the store."

"You saw a big man? Could you identify him?"

The boy shook his head. "It was dark. The car was only there a minute. The woman got out to hold the door open for the guy to get in fast. Then they drove off real quick."

Damn! "That was all you saw? You're sure?"

He nodded. "Except the big guy had a gray suit, and the woman had a green dress and real dark hair kind of long, and the car was a blue Mercedes four-door."

I stared. "You saw all that in the dark?"

"Sure," the boy said. "When the woman got out of the car I looked close 'cause it might have been Mr. Castro, see? She walked around in front of the head-lights and I saw she was a woman. I mean, I saw the guy's suit and the woman and the color of the car because I was looking hard for Mr. Castro."

Stood in the dark of that empty street, near that deserted building site, and looked closely at two people for only a few seconds. Because he wanted to give a package to a man who had forgotten it in his store. A man who had been nice to him. A man he had gotten

184

to like. So he looked hard, hoping one of the people was Mr. Castro, but the man was too big and had on a gray suit, and the other was a woman in a green dress, and the car was a dark-blue Mercedes, and ...

In the office Pearce looked at his drawn shades as if he were seeing the city invisible on the other side. Schatz looked at the door as if he wished he were on the other side going away.

"Castro didn't need a razor," I said. "So when he was delayed that night, he hurried a little and forgot the package."

"It's not much, Dan," Pearce said.

"The boy can't really identify either of them," Schatz said. "He didn't get the license number of the car, and you got any idea how many dark-blue Mercedes there are in the city?"

"It's enough," I said. "The woman walked in her own headlight beams. A slim, dark-haired woman in a green dress, and that fits Susan Roth and what she was wearing according to ten witnesses at the Junior League. The man fits Roth and what he was wearing. Susan Roth's car is a dark-blue Mercedes."

Pearce shook his head. "I don't know, Dan."

"With what I dug up on all their actions, their motives, my reconstruction of what happened, it'll probably convince a jury."

"Probably?" Pearce said.

"You want to tell the DA about *probably*, Fortune?" Schatz said.

I said, "Probably is all we'll need."

And the interoffice telephone rang. Pearce answered.

"She's here," the captain said.

The door opened and Susan Roth, formerly Susan Castro, stepped into the room. She stood tall and poised, a fine-looking woman. Still young and close to beautiful. Her cool eyes took in each of us in turn.

"Sit down, Mrs. Roth," Captain Pearce said.

"Am I under arrest, Captain?"

"No," Pearce said, "not yet. But Mr. Fortune there has a story we think you should hear."

Her eyes turned to look at me. She looked at my empty sleeve and my old tweed sport jacket and cords. Her lips curled faintly. She did not think much of me, but she sat down, waited, her foot swinging lightly in its two-hundred-dollar pump.

I told my story. From my first hunch about Castro and his murder plan, through what I had pieced together about Roth and her plan, to Castro's mistake and the soda fountain boy, and her walking through the beams of the headlights. She showed no reaction until the soda fountain boy. At her careless walk through the headlights she blinked. At Roth coming out of the building site in his gray suit, her foot stopped swinging.

"Castro's company hired me to investigate his murder, Mrs. Roth. They'll do everything they can to convict you and your husband. They've seen my report, they've already hired the best lawyers to work with the DA. Since you didn't kill Castro yourself, the captain there can offer you a deal to turn state witness. Accessory, five-to-ten years. With good behavior, parole in as little as three years. Maybe less. If you stand up in court with Roth, you could get life without parole."

Her face showed nothing. I was going on my judgment, on everything I had learned, sensed, in the killer's mind of Susan Roth. With both Castro and Roth out of the way, her sons would be rich boys. She would know how to get her share. In prison for life, what good would the money do her? What I had guessed, uncovered, pieced together might not convince a jury. She might get off. On the other hand, she might not. Say a fifty-fifty chance, maybe a little worse. I figured those odds would be enough for Susan Roth.

"Charge me first"—her voice had no emotion— "then I'll tell you how Norman killed poor Maxwell."

It wasn't what should have happened, but it was something. The murder had been mostly her idea, she should have taken the big fall. It's an imperfect world; you get what you can.

The case had been all a matter of getting inside their killer minds. Norman Roth would never make the deal, turn her in. Susan Roth, once Susan Castro, would and did. She was a practical woman.

It Was a Hard Fall

HAROLD WALLS

Harold Walls is a pseudonym. He describes him-self as a "dyspeptic misanthrope with no real de-sire to reveal my identity or my motive in writing fiction to the world at large. That's why I write under a pseudonym."

IT WAS CALLED the Celebrity Club, but the closest thing to a celebrity that had ever sipped stale, warm beer from a chipped bar glass at Johnny-O's joint was Marblehead Dexter Simpkins, especially the night before his picture was on the front page of the *Jamestown Journal* as the prime-and-just-apprehended suspect in the rape and murder and then mutilation of the fourteen-year-old daughter of a very prominent man-about-town who just happened to be a white accountant, public and certified.

Marblehead's rise to fame in the city at large was meteoric, but he has faded from memory fast. He is scheduled to make the front page one more time about four years from now, when his appeals run out and he gets to choose three witnesses to his untimely and unnatural demise. One way or the other, Elgin Balfour means to be there.

Marblehead was the main man to the Celebrity Club regulars, who still talk, three years later, about how he got framed. And the man had such promise, such talent, such style, they say. They remembered when Marblehead played football, and oh, how he dived into that line—head first and feet driving, never stopping till he was down, and even then always grinning like he had the world by the balls and knew just when to squeeze. He was just biding his time, they all said then.

Marblehead Simpkins used to walk like a king through Roosevelt Village, and the boys stood back and the girls came forth and Marblehead showed the girls that he was the man, their man. He was six-feet-four of prime fullbacking scholarship meat, wrapped in proud and shining ebony the year he left high school. That was the summer a going-on-drunk rent-a-cop caught Marblehead behind the concession stand by the football field one moonlit night, his shiny black ass pumping and glistening between the unshaven legs and turned-down toes of Marissa Balfour, who didn't practice discrimination and never stopped screaming that she wanted it all, till it was all gone.

Marblehead wanted her to have it, too, but the DA felt their desires were improper and that the man had to learn some humility, or at least discretion, even if he was just eighteen and Big-Ten-bound, so he put the boy's ass in the can for two to ten on a charge of rape statutorily. There he could ponder what might have been if Marissa's daddy, Elgin, had his way.

"You're gonna have to get used to white boys from now on, son." The bailiff laughed, and Marissa cried, because Elgin was sending her north to get her head straight and her ass in line in a place where the moon might as well never rise and the sun might as well never shine.

Marblehead emerged from stir a changed man. "I used to be the best-dressed motherfucker in Roosevelt Village, before I learned to spend my cash making my body feel good instead of look good," he used to say after they set him free. And Marblehead knew how to feel good when he came back to Jamestown. Speed-balls, red devils, white magic, and soul dust, 99 percent pure. Mainlined, streamlined, down-the-hatch, and gone. Marblehead took it the way it came. And he learned that every front door has a silver lining, especially if you go in through the back, real quiet, when nobody's home. A man with a habit has got to cop seven days a week, every week of the year.

Big appetites don't attract attention at the Celebrity Club, but Marblehead's hungers left the regulars in awe. It took twenty-four long-neck bottles of Miller

High Life beer, two long-legged, pelvis-pumping sugar plums, and one pop every four hours of vein-warming glory dust to keep Marblehead satisfied, each day, every day, and he got mean when he wasn't satisfied.

That's how he came to fall hard. He got mean when he should have been patient, and talked when he should have listened, and he forgot that you don't have to be big to get revenge. Like Papa Monk Sanders says, "You fuck over a man that's got balls, and you better kill him, because beating him's not enough." Elgin Balfour's got balls like tangerines.

Marblehead's rise to the heights of celebrity, his subsequent fall, and his understanding of the wisdom Papa Monk spoke began at 7:00 A.M. Thursday morning, August 13, 1981. Marblehead was having the first beer and third cigarette of the day, standing outside the Celebrity watching the honkies motor officeward down Chesnutt Street. He felt bad. Sherrille Ann Cleveland—Pucker Puss, she was called in the Village—had kicked his ass out of bed. The cost of her affection came high, and Marblehead was short the price that night because his coffers were close to bare and he could cop for one, but not two. "You want to light my fire, you come back with the fuel," Puss said firmly, and she turned her man out into the street.

It was all a matter of coincidence that morning that Marblehead flipped his butt just a little too hard; and Elgin Balfour drove by just a little too slow; and the window of the 98 Oldsmobile, four-door deluxe with luxury package was down just a little too far; and Marissa was in the front seat, just back from boarding-school-and-locked-room exile; and that still-lit butt landed in the lap of her pretty, off-white, not-quite-virgin silk dress; and—well—there was smoke where there used to be fire.

Marissa screamed, and Elgin slammed on the brakes, and Marblehead didn't notice, because he felt too bad, until Elgin Balfour stood, his nose six inches from the gold medallion around Marblehead's neck and spit out a threat: "You're going to be sorry, boy."

Marblehead said, "Ain't nothing stinks like Listerine and Jade East cheek by jowl, so would you get outta my face?" And he laughed like a man without a care in the world and looked at Marissa and said, "Hey, baby, long time no see." Spitting in the wind.

Elgin pronounced a death sentence and left. Marblehead adjusted his dick and had another beer. He had his day to plan, opportunities in suburbia to explore.

This day Marblehead would be a plumber's helper. He took off his gold and put on his old clothes. He borrowed for $50 an about-to-be-painted pickup from Shine Like New Auto Repaint, and stole into the bright morning of Quail Pointe Estates, shovel rattling in the back. He had a rag in one pocket, a bag in the other, a beer in his fist, and Puss on his mind. When he found a house that looked just right, he parked his truck in front and dug a hole in back—by the flower garden. That was just for show, while he waited to see if some busybody housewife, bored with soaps and call-in-to-win radio, would spoil his day. Forty-five minutes of digging, and Marblehead was ready to work.

He wrapped his rag around the end of that shovel

like a craftsman, and broke a windowpane so skillfully that even he didn't hear it shatter. He climbed inside, dirt-clogged feet first, gave himself a pop, and started separating the dross from the gold, as they say.

Marblehead was a careful man, but quick about his business, and inside of an hour, he was out and grinning, on his way to liquidate his assets. He left behind a dirt-stained hand-knotted Persian rug that drove the lady of the house to trembling, fearsome fury, and an unfilled hole in a zoysia carpet outside that cut to the quick of her husband's soul. Never mind insured losses of $18,384.98, replacement value covered. State Farm paid that. A fence named Mouse the Mule paid Marblehead seven bills even and the matter was closed.

The main man went hunting sweet, soulful solace at Puss Cleveland's, his pockets bulging. She lifted his burden and relieved his tension, hauled his ashes and stoked his furnace before they went to the Celebrity to party. Drinks were on the man; that's how a celebrity acts at Fifth and Chesnutt. And that's why a roomful of gentlemen of leisure and ladies of the evening know damn well that Dexter aka Marblehead Simpkins perpetrated neither rape nor the least degree of assault, not to mention mutilation, on anybody fairer than sweet, dark chocolate, more or less the shade of Puss Cleveland, that night.

But somebody did.

And he left his mess in Elgin Balfour's backyard.

Screaming and yelling, weeping and wailing were the Friday-morning sounds on Chesnutt Street when four carloads of determined young officers of the law, shotguns loaded and billy clubs drawn, descended on one slightly buzzing ex-fullback who could not comprehend their anger. They dragged him off fighting to await the opportunity to plead his case before the bar of justice. A speedy trial was his right, and Elgin saw to his rights.

"I didn't do no wrong," the man lied, but we knew what he meant.

"Fry his ass," Elgin Balfour cried.

"I saw Dexter Simpkins in the vicinity of the crime," Marissa Balfour wept spitefully; "he tried to get me, but daddy scared him off.

"He was with me and fifteen others at the Celebrity," Puss Cleveland countered.

"You're a whore, and reliable witnesses don't frequent that haven for the lawless," the DA replied.

"You're a nubbin-dicked piece of shit," Johnny-O piped up.

"You're in contempt," the judge declared. "Order in the court."

The jury said guilty in the first degree.

"Fry his ass, Judge. You owe it to the community," Elgin Balfour demanded.

The judge concurred, Elgin winked. A hod carrier named Andrew breathed a sigh of relief. And that settled it.

The night of the judgment there was a mournful gathering at the Celebrity Club. Puss Cleveland sobbed and bought for the house, courtesy of her used-to-be old man, and they drank to his honor.

"We were gonna get married," Puss announced, tears swelling up in her eyes.

"Be glad you didn't," Johnny-O allowed, lust swelling up in his pants.

Papa Monk Sanders said, "The boy had it coming. He was predesigned for a big fall. But Lord, he knew how to act at party time."

And they drank one more bottle of beer to his memory.

Subscription to THE NEW BLACK MASK
     $27.80/year in the U.S.

Subscription correspondence should be sent to
     THE NEW BLACK MASK
     129 West 56th Street
     New York, NY 10019